GW00866497

Albeson and the Germans

It seems a very simple thing that starts off all the trouble – a rumour that two German children are coming to Church Street School. Although the teachers cannot understand the panic that this causes, Albeson can. His comics, and his dead grandfather, have taught him all about Germans. And he doesn't fancy the idea one little bit.

The plan that Albeson's friend Pam comes up with frightens him stiff. Unfortunately, his mate Smithie, who's very tough and sometimes a bit odd, likes the idea. So Albeson has no choice. From then on, everything Albeson does gets him deeper and deeper into trouble, and, finally, danger.

Also available in Fontana Lions

TWISTERS *Ed. Steve Bowles*
GRIMM GRANGE *William Browning*
TIG'S CRIME *T. R. Burch*
A QUESTION OF COURAGE *Marjorie Darke*
THE NEW NOAH *Gerald Durrell*
NOBODY'S FAMILY IS GOING TO CHANGE *Louise Fitzhugh*
PRIVATE, KEEP OUT! *Gwen Grant*
KNOCK AND WAIT *Gwen Grant*
WHEN HITLER STOLE PINK RABBIT *Judith Kerr*
THE FIB AND OTHER STORIES *George Layton*
THE THIRD CLASS GENIE *Robert Leeson*
HAROLD AND BELLA, JAMMY AND ME *Robert Leeson*
GRANGE HILL RULES – OK? *Robert Leeson*
THE SIZE SPIES *Jan Needle*
MY MATE SHOFIQ *Jan Needle*
THE SILVER CROWN *Robert O'Brien*

Albeson and the Germans

by

JAN NEEDLE

FONTANA · LIONS

First published 1977 by Andre Deutsch Ltd.
First published in Fontana Lions 1981
by William Collins Sons & Co Ltd
14 St James's Place, London SW1

Copyright © 1977 by Jan Needle

Printed in Great Britain
by William Collins Sons & Co Ltd, Glasgow

CONDITIONS OF SALE
This book is sold subject to the condition
that it shall not, by way of trade or otherwise,
be lent, re-sold, hired out or otherwise circulated
without the publisher's prior consent in any form of
binding or cover other than that in which it is
published and without a similar condition
including this condition being imposed
on the subsequent purchaser.

For my Mother
and Father

Chapter 1

If Albeson had gone to school that morning, he would have heard that the Germans were coming 'straight from the horse's mouth' as his mother would say. But it was Monday, and the sun was shining very hard, and it was the morning of the spelling test. Albeson had lost quite a lot of sleep the night before, worrying about the spelling test. So when he saw Smithie lurking by the graveyard gates he felt his heart jump. He was not allowed to play with Smithie any more; but Smithie was lurking in the gateway in the shadow of the chapel, waiting to pounce.

Albeson scuffed his feet in the gutter and walked slower and slower as he got near the gates. He didn't look at Smithie, but he knew he was being watched. He'd been told a lot by Mrs Armstrong not to talk to Smithie, and his dad had already thumped him once. Well, he wouldn't talk. Not unless he was spoken to.

''Allo, Albeson, what are you doin'?'

Albeson stopped and looked up at Smithie's round freckled face. He had a red nose, a bit, and a sore on his lip. He always had a sore lip, and Pam said it would be the death of him. It amazed Albeson that someone who was only waiting to die could be so cheerful about it. But he'd never dared mention it to Smithie. Smithie was very big — much bigger than Albeson — and could get rough.

'Lost your tongue have you? Where you going?'

'Where do you think? School aren't I? Got a spelling

7

test.' Albeson kicked at the iron gate. Well, Smithie spoke first, he thought, that was one thing.

'School on a day like this? You're barmy. I'm going down . . .' Smithie broke off and grinned. 'Eh, come off it, Albeson, you can't even read!'

Albeson kicked harder at the gate. He noticed that the toe of his plimsoll was coming away from the sole so he worked on it, trying to concentrate on tearing the canvas although he felt his face going red.

'Shut up then, Smithie. That's why I'm going to school isn't it?'

Smithie laughed. Suddenly his big knuckly hand shot out and hovered under Albeson's nose. In it were three coins. Two tens and a fifty.

'Got your bathers? I've got mine.' He patted a bulge in his jacket pocket. 'I'm going down Flathouse for a swim. You coming? I've got money.'

Albeson's heart leaped. Good old Smithie. He always got some money somewhere even though he didn't go to school and he didn't work. Flathouse Creek, a swim. He looked up at the sun and it hurt his eyes. Spelling test!

'Where did you get it? Did you nick it?'

'No, me Uncle Frank gave it to me didn't he? I did him some jobs. Cleared away the old flowers off the graves.' He jerked his thumb over his shoulder towards the cemetery. 'Makes people buy more don't it? So he gave me this.'

It was good having a mate like Smithie. His Uncle Frank kept the flower shop on the estate, just a couple of hundred yards from the cemetery. Albeson and Smithie often used to walk among the stones, gathering up dead and dying flowers to make way for more and improve Uncle Frank's trade. That way Albeson got to know the graves and wander among the dead. He'd never have dared if they hadn't had to for Uncle Frank. Smithie nodded towards the bus stop at the end of the street.

'You coming then? We'll play on the logs and have a swim. Be good, it will.'

'Haven't got me bathers though,' said Albeson. He knew he ought to go to school, but he knew he wasn't going to. It was only a token protest. Who needed bathers?

'Who needs bathers then?' said Smithie. 'Got your pants on haven't you? Used them before haven't you? Getting shy in your old age?'

'Seventy p' mused Albeson. 'Here, Smithie, will you buy us an ice-cream?'

'Course I will, you 'nana. What d'you want, white or pink?'

It was a deal.

The bus was an old Leyland Atlantean and jerked and bounced in the way that Albeson loved. Smithie said it was something to do with the gearbox, but he didn't seem too sure. But they both liked to watch the way the driver made the bus lurch forward by pushing the little knobbed lever in its funny box by the steering wheel. They sat in the long seat near the front, on the pavement side, with their feet in the gangway. Lots of people got on and off, and they spent the ride guessing which ones were holiday-makers and secretly sneering at them.

'My dad says they're a rotten nuisance,' said Albeson. 'If they stayed in their own towns there wouldn't be such a rotten mess in this one. He says he can't hardly get home from the Dockyard at night now 'cause there's so much traffic, and he's only got a bike.'

'They bring money in though,' Smithie said. 'They helps the . . . the local . . . Well, they bring in their money and spend it. That's what Uncle Frank says anyway.'

'Don't see that it helps him though,' Albeson giggled. 'Don't get many holiday-makers dying off and needing flowers, do you?'

'More's the pity!' Smithie shouted.

They doubled up with laughter and banged each other on the back until the conductor told them to shut up or get off. Then they tried to be quiet, but kept having muffled bursts through their closed mouths. They got off at the 'Air Balloon' and rolled about on the pavement until they saw a gap in the traffic and darted across the road, the joke forgotten.

'Got to be careful down here nowadays,' Smithie whispered as they got close to Flathouse. 'They've started using dogs to patrol. They're alsations, trained to kill. And the men have got orders to let 'em.'

Albeson's heart sank. Up till now they'd never been bothered at Flathouse. The men working on the timber boats didn't seem to mind a couple of boys larking around.

'Why's that then, Smithie? I thought they didn't care down here. There's nothing to nick.'

Smithie was scornful. 'Nothing to nick? What about all that wood then? What about all them planks? There's wood down here worth thousands. Millions!'

'Yeah, but no one's going to pinch it, are they? I mean there's too much of it. You couldn't take a pocketful could you?'

Smithie looked at him darkly, his moon face secretive.

'There's been a gang,' he said. 'Coming in at the dead of night with great lorries. They've been nicking it by the ton. There's been a murder too, they reckon.'

Albeson looked around him a bit fearfully. Flathouse looked just the same. Mountains of cut timber lying on the quays waiting to be moved, smelling fresh and sweet. Two freighters lying alongside on the opposite jetty, one half-unloaded, the other still with a deck cargo of clean white wood piled almost up to her bridge windows. One or two men in overalls wandering about the dockside taking no notice of them. A crane over the half-unloaded ship buzzing and throbbing in the early heat. He heard a dog bark.

'Listen,' said Smithie. 'That's one of 'em! A German sheep dog with dripping jaws! We'd better go careful!'

'German sheep dog? You said they were alsatians,' said Albeson. His mouth had gone dry. He stared about him.

'Alsatians *are* German sheep dogs, you ghost,' said Smithie. 'Don't you know nothing?'

'Here, do you think we ought to clear off?' said Albeson. He didn't like Germans, he'd heard about them from his grandpa. Alsatians, which had always seemed pretty dangerous animals, suddenly got much more dangerous. He licked his lips.

Smithie was delighted. His face caught the sun and shone like a plate as he nodded his head up and down. His mop of sandy, wild hair danced in Albeson's eyes.

'You're scared ain't you! I've got you scared haven't I? Little Albeson wants his mum!'

Albeson screwed up his face and scowled.

'Ah shut up then, Smithie. Briar Boys don't get scared that easy!'

'Briar Boys! You ain't a Briar Boy, you're a Briar kid. You wait till I tell your Derek. He's a Briar Boy. He'll thump you one.'

'You watch it, Smithie, that's all. Even the nippers on Briar are tough. Flower shop kid! Smithie lives in a flower shop! Smithie lives in a flower shop!'

Smithie made a dive at him and Albeson nipped out of the way behind a pile of timber. They chased and larked about for quite a while, shrieking and laughing. Finally they ran down to the greasy pebble beach that dipped deeply into the murky waters of the creek, where the seaweed-covered logs lay chained together in the harbour. They flopped down against an old packing case, panting.

'Anyway,' Albeson said at last, 'I may be only a Briar kid but it's still the toughest street on the estate. All the rest's rubbish. I bet you wish you lived there.'

'Don't you worry about me,' said Smithie. 'I'm tough enough. I come from Hillside before we moved to town. They're hard there too. That's how I had my accident, sledging up at Hillside.'

Albeson had heard the story before, but it still made his stomach go tight to think about it. He knew it was true. The kids on Hillside were mad. They'd do anything. They had the hill at the back of them, with chalk-pits and old forts and electricity pylons to climb. Lots of them got killed bird-nesting and thieving, and they roamed around in gangs. Even Briar Boys thought twice about starting a brickfight with the Hillside lot.

In the winter, when it snowed, lots of kids from all over went up the hill to sledge, whether on the real thing or on old trays and bits of plastic it didn't matter. But the Hillside boys thought that was too soft. They built their sledge runs on the steep streets of the estate – long, icy tracks that wove in and out of the lamp posts and parked cars. They went down headfirst, steering with their feet, and reached speeds that were enough to make you die of fright.

'I can still remember it like it was yesterday,' Smithie was saying. 'I was going about a hundred mile an hour I reckon. I'd come all the way down Churchill and I was just swinging round to go up the slope in Wingfield and slow down. Then this car come out of Staunton Street, right across me. I slewed round to the right, then the left, then I spun right round and found myself going towards the main road. It was so fast I didn't know what'd happened. My nose was about an inch off the ground and I'd wrenched my shoe off. All my toenails were out they said later.'

Albeson watched Smithie's big moon face with its funny lop-sided smile. He was fascinated. He couldn't take his eyes away. He seemed to see his friend racing down the ice at breakneck speed towards disaster. At the bottom of the steep street the main road. Its lights rushed closer and closer, the cars and lorries whizzed across it.

'There was a milk-van parked near the bottom. It was the only thing before the road. So I aimed at its back tyre, to stop me.' Smithie's eyes closed and his lips twitched a little. His smile got broader, more crooked. Albeson was panting, although he knew what Smithie was going to say.

'I hit the tyre with my shoulder,' said Smithie. 'This one.' He touched his left shoulder, drooping under the padding in his old check sports jacket. 'Bang! Away goes the sledge in one direction and up into the air goes me. Funny, I remember it although I was going like a cartwheel, so fast. I saw the lights, and the road, and the shops all spinning, just like it was slow motion, turning in front of me.' He paused. 'Didn't see the lamp post though.' He opened his eyes. 'Didn't half give me a clout, Albeson. I was in hospital nearly a year.'

Albeson's stomach was like water. The story always horrified him; made him afraid. He wouldn't have done it, not for anything. Smithie was mad, no doubt about it. But he was a hero too.

'You asleep then, nipper?' Albeson jerked his head up. Smithie was standing before him in his funny old woollen bathing costume. He was quite brown and had a chain round his neck. 'Come on, get ready. Race you out across the logs.'

The logs, stained and dripping and rough to the bare feet, stretched out across the waters of the creek like a half-sunk platform. They were chained together, with sea between each one and weed hanging from the bottoms of them all, and the boys ran roaring out to the very edge, where the thin ends dipped and sank as you stood on them. Every now and again they'd fall in and swim around a bit, although not for long, because Smithie said there were conger eels hiding among the logs, and if one of those got its teeth into you it was a well-known fact that you were a goner. He also said you'd to keep your mouth tightly shut when you were swimming, because you could get TB if you swallowed sea-water. Albeson didn't know exactly what TB was, but he certainly didn't want it. And he knew Smithie was right because his mother also said it was dangerous to swim at Flathouse.

Later, as they lay baking in the sun on the gently-moving platform of logs, Albeson thought of his mother again.

'Hey, Smithie,' he said. 'My old lady would half kill me if she knew I was here with you.'

'Why's that then?' asked Smithie.

Albeson opened his mouth to speak then shut it with a snap. He didn't dare to say it really, that he wasn't meant to play with him. Smithie heard his teeth click.

'What you doing, Albeson? Catching flies?'

'Nah. Going to have a kip that's all. Hey, Smithie?'

'Yeah?'

'Better than school this is, any day. Fan-tastic!'

'Albeson,' said Smithie. 'You've hit the nail right on the head!'

Chapter 2

By the end of the long afternoon Albeson's chest and legs were red, he was hungry and thirsty, and he was better off to the tune of a toy lorry. He was hungry – practically starving – because it was well after four and he'd only had an ice-cream and a raspberry bun all day. He sat on the Briar Road bomb-site, so that he could keep an eye on his front door to see when Mrs Armstrong left, and drove the shining new truck in and out of the weeds, loaded with carefully broken chunks of brick.

He didn't have his mind on the game much, however, although he fancied being a lorry driver when he grew up, because of Mrs Armstrong. It had been a shock to see her going into his house with Deena as he'd turned into Briar on his way home, and he was a little scared.

Mrs Armstrong was Albeson's teacher, not Deena's, although she'd been pulling his sister along by her hand, trying to stop her bawling at the same time. No, the reason for the visit was obvious. Albeson had played truant, and Mrs Armstrong had come along to see something was done about it. He felt the back of his neck tingle. He'd been skipping school quite a bit what with one thing and another, and his father was a dab hand with the belt.

Smithie had slouched off home after he'd been into Woolie's to get Albeson the lorry. He looked funny, big and stooping with his hair stiff and wild from the dried salt in it.

People said rotten things about Smithie, he was not much liked, but he was generous all right.

After Albeson had had a little kip on the logs and they'd eaten their ice-cream and cake dinner, they'd got on a bus to the Camber. This was the commercial dock that they liked the best, and they stood for a couple of hours watching the mobile cranes unloading spuds and caulies and tomatoes from the lovely little freighters. Smithie reckoned he was going to join the Navy when he grew up, and he was a bit scornful about the little cargo boats, but Albeson loved them. Smithie read the names off the sterns for him, and where they came from. He also told him what the different coloured flags meant.

Their favourite boat, that even Smithie reckoned was as good as anything in the Navy, was a small black-hulled general cargo boat called the *Carrie*, from Newcastle. She didn't fly the Red Ensign, but a different flag altogether. This was called a houseflag, Smithie explained, and showed which shipping line she belonged to. She visited the Camber quite often, and Albeson always liked it best when she was there, with her high, proud bow and streamlined red funnel.

'Where's the *Carrie* today I wonder,' he'd said. 'Haven't seen her for a couple of weeks.'

'Ah she'll be abroad I shouldn't wonder,' Smithie replied. 'Over in America, or Russia or somewhere. Eh, that's what I call living, nipper. Keep your lorries for me. I'll be on a destroyer soon, sailing the Seven Seas, shooting up the enemy.'

'Well that's hard luck for you then,' said Albeson, ''cause we haven't got an enemy, so who're you going to blow up then?'

Smithie jumped on him and jerked his arm up his back. Albeson screamed in agony, but Smithie went on pulling, higher and higher, laughing like mad. When he saw that Albeson was crying he suddenly let go and was very sorry. He put his arm round him, and although Albeson tried to push him away he couldn't even break his hold. That was the trouble with Smithie. He didn't know his own strength and he could be very rough.

Albeson was still sniffing on the bus home, when Smithie suddenly grabbed him and pulled him off two stops early as the doors were closing and the bus was moving off. They were outside Woolworths.

'You wait there, Albeson,' said Smithie. 'I won't be long.'

'Go to hell,' said Albeson. 'I'm going home, you big bully.'

'You wait there or I'll break your other arm. I'm going to get you something ain't I?'

After five minutes Albeson had begun to get frightened. He was wondering if he dared run home when Smithie appeared and hurried him along the pavement. There was a bulge under his crazy old jacket. When they'd almost reached Briar he stopped.

'Here you are, nipper. I bought you this. I didn't mean to hurt you, honest.'

He thrust the lorry into Albeson's hands and walked off, his left shoulder drooping. It was a Foden flat truck, with real chains round the back. Just what the doctor ordered.

The stained red door to Albeson's house opened jerkily – it had a broken panel and always stuck – and Mrs Armstrong came out. Albeson ducked behind a bush as she looked up and down the street, then watched her as she made for the main road. Mrs Armstrong was nice and he felt a bit sorry that he'd played truant. But he felt even sorrier she'd come home to tell his mum about it. There'd be a row for sure. He thought for a moment about staying out till bedtime, but his stomach was having none of it. Row or no row he had to get in there and eat.

The noise as he reached the still-open front door was even louder than usual. Deena was screaming her head off, the television was up loud, and his mum was shouting over them both. Albeson had sneaked in quietly and was heading for the kitchen when he heard a sound that frightened him sick. He turned back towards the front door in a panic, but he was too late. The passage door swung open and his dad came

17

out, shirt-sleeves flapping, holding the newspaper, furiously angry. He was looking over his shoulder into the room and shouting.

'Get her off to bed, that's all! "The Germans are coming, the Germans are coming!" I'll give her Germans!'

He walked straight into Albeson, who was frantically trying to hide the lorry, and they both sprawled against the wall. As Albeson fell the truck rolled along the passage into a pile of shoes. He felt a flood of relief as it disappeared.

'What are you playing at, you fool,' said his father, staggering to keep his balance. 'Lurking in the passage like that, you could have killed me. Get out of it!'

Albeson jumped to obey, and was scuttling towards the sitting-room when his father grabbed his arm, the one Smithie had hurt.

'Hey, not so fast! Why weren't you at school today, you little cheat?'

Why weren't you at work, thought Albeson bitterly, but he kept his mouth shut.

'Come on, sonny boy, why weren't you at school? Where were you skiving off to? I've had your teacher round this afternoon and I reckon you're about ready for a dose of this.'

Albeson gulped as his father hooked his thumb into his leather belt, near the buckle. Trouble was, he couldn't think of anything to say. There was a renewed burst of wailing from behind the door, then the sound of a slap. His mother appeared, red-faced, with Deena in tow. His little sister had wet cheeks and a running nose and her cardigan was torn.

His mother said: 'You heard what your daddy told you. Any more out of you, Miss, and it's straight to bed.'

Deena's face crumpled up and she opened her mouth.

'I'm scared of Germans I am!' she shrieked. 'I'm scared of Germans!'

There was a flurry of slaps and she was shot upstairs in a whirl of arms and legs. Dad jerked his head at Albeson.

'Go on,' he said. 'You too, I've had enough of the both of you. Get to bed and keep your mouth shut or I'll belt the living daylights out of you. And if you play truant once more, just once more, you'll know it. All right?'

Albeson nodded dumbly. He shot a glance at the pile of shoes. The cab of the lorry was sticking up like a green island in the dirty jumble, but he could do nothing. He was starving hungry too, but that was also hard luck. His mother came downstairs as he started to climb.

'Germans!' he heard her say to dad. 'I just don't know where she gets her nonsense from. Germans!'

He went upstairs thoughtfully, with a sort of excited feeling in his empty stomach. What was up with Deena then, going on like that? Maybe it was not a bad thing after all, being sent to bed at 5 o'clock.

It was very hot and sticky in the bedroom, with the sun shining through the thin curtains as brightly as if they hadn't been there. Outside the usual row of Briar went on as if nothing had happened, dogs barking, kids shouting, cars going up and down. There was a blow-fly trapped between the window glass and the curtains, filling the room with a heavy buzzing. Deena's muffled sobs came thick and fast from under the pile of blankets on her bed.

Before the council put the inside toilets in the houses along Briar Avenue, Albeson had had a bedroom to himself. Now there was a room less (not counting the new bathroom of course) so he had to share with Deena. It seemed daft to him really, because he'd much preferred the outside lav anyway, especially in summer, and his family didn't use the bath much, not being used to it. His big brothers, Derek and Alan, shared the other small bedroom across the upstairs passage.

He undressed down to his vest and pants and wiggled his dirty toes. He'd picked up a lot of tar and oil down at Flathouse. Pity it was so mucky, because it was such good fun. The clean beaches, where everyone else went, the holiday-makers and so on, were no good at all. There was nothing to do except chuck stones, and you soon got stopped if you started.

19

Albeson rolled onto his bed and jerked the covers about so that they weren't bunched up under him. He looked at the big rain-stain on the ceiling, listening to Deena's sobs. Not too long now, he thought. He was a good judge of his sister's squalling fits. If he left it too long she'd go out like a light and be fast asleep. If he spoke to her too soon it would set her off again like a runaway train. When the gap between each sniff was just right he rolled over and touched where he guessed her shoulder to be.

'Hey, Deen, what's up then?'

The bundle of bedclothes wriggled as though she was trying to shrug off his hand. Albeson waited. No more sobs, just a few sniffles.

'Hey, Deen,' he said. 'What lies at the bottom of the sea and shivers and shakes? Eh?'

The sniffs stopped. Suddenly the blankets heaved and Deena's tear-stained face, bright red and glowing, appeared. Couldn't resist a riddle, Deena couldn't.

'I don't know.'

'A nervous wreck! Get it?'

She didn't of course. Deena never got his jokes, but she'd stopped crying at any rate. He thought carefully about what to say next.

'You hungry are you? I am. I've only had an ice-cream today. And a cake. I'm starved.'

Deena propped herself up on to her elbow and looked at him as if he'd done a murder.

'Why wasn't you at school today? You're a bad boy. You can't read and you're older than me.'

Albeson made a funny noise to show what he thought of school. 'Dah, school. It's a dump. It's for little girls and cissies school is. Anyway . . .' he made his face blank, as though he wasn't really interested . . . 'Anyway, what happened at school that's so special?'

For a moment he thought Deena was going to start up again. Her eyes went round and her mouth quivered.

'Whee, Jimmy,' she said. 'It's awful. The Germans are

coming. They're coming to our school. Now there'll be some fights!'

'What do you mean, coming? What Germans? What are you talking about?'

'Miss Gumley said. At prayers. Two of 'em a brother and a sister. Coming to the school. And Jimmy . . .' Her voice dropped to a frightened whisper . . . 'They can't speak English. They can only speak German. Binnsie said . . . Binnsie said they eat people!'

Albeson lay on his back and stared at the ceiling. His heart fluttered. Of course they ate people, it was a well-known fact. He knew all about Germans, he knew them inside out and backwards. Brutal-faced men in square helmets who spoke in funny writing and called English soldiers rude names. In the comics they always lost in the end, and of course they lost the war. But there was grandad to think about. Grandad had been in the war and the Germans had captured him. Grandad had a wooden leg and he used to thrill and terrify Albeson with his stories. Oh yes, Germans ate people. Grandad had said so many times.

'Are they going in the babies?' he asked. 'Is that what all the row was about when I came in? Is that why Mrs Armstrong brought you home?'

Deena got sulky. She wouldn't tell what had happened, except that the Germans were older than her. They might even be in Albeson's class. But as the juniors and the infants were in the same school it didn't matter. She could still be eaten along with the rest of them. Binnsie had said they'd rather eat babies anyway. Albeson felt sick. In his class. It was awful.

'Tell us some more what Mrs Gumley said.' There was no answer. 'Deena. Deen! What else did she say? Eh?'

Deena was asleep, with her mouth open and her bottom in the air. No use trying to wake her up, she'd sleep through a thunderstorm. Albeson felt his stomach churning. The Germans were coming. Now there'd be some fights!

Chapter 3

Next morning Albeson felt much worse about the Germans. He had slept for a long time, some of it in the hot, light evening, some of it during the hot uncomfortable night. But he had slept very badly, and he had had terrible dreams. Men in grey uniforms, with Saturday morning pictures faces, had chased him, yelling bloodthirsty yells and waving long pig-sticker bayonets from the ends of their devilish-looking rifles.

After Deena had gone to sleep he'd lain on his back on the rumpled bed staring up at the damp-stain. As he watched it had become the face of a German, square-headed and evil. Albeson, half-asleep, thought of his grandad.

Grandad had died last year, but Albeson could still picture him very clearly. He was a short man with a stubbly chin and a mouth made yellow from years and years of smoking cigarettes down to the stubs. He glued the cigarette to his lower lip and breathed and spoke without moving it. As he talked little showers of sparks came from the end of the fag, and as he breathed he sucked smoke straight into his nostrils, then out again. He coughed a lot and sometimes he blinked or even cried because of the shortness of the stub and the heat of the end. He would have burnt his lips, too, but the wetness creeping outwards always damped the cigarette down at just the right moment. Then he spat out the yellow end and lit another. It amazed Albeson to see his grandad smoke. It seemed so uncomfortable, so dirty. In the end, his mother said, it had killed him.

The next most fascinating thing about grandad, to Albeson, was his wooden leg. He liked to sit on his knee, the wooden one, and feel the hardness. Grandad let him tap it with his knuckles. It was very queer. Albeson would rap rap at grandad's wooden leg, then pinch his real one. Grandad would laugh, and cough, and Albeson's face would disappear in a cloud of smoke and sparks.

The leg had gone in the war. Grandad had been rear gunner in a bomber, and one day he'd been shot down over Germany by a fighter, when Albeson's dad had been just a little kid. He'd parachuted down but the fighter had followed. His dog-end would quiver with rage as he spat out his hatred, and Albeson shared it with him, wishing that he could catch the pilot and do terrible things to him, torture him and hurt him and kill him. For he'd followed grandad down, firing with his machine guns.

'Shot my leg to pieces, the swine. Shot my leg to pieces. Jimmy – never trust the Boche, not ever. Followed me down and shot my leg to pieces.'

It seemed so desperately cruel. Here was his grandad, father to Albeson's father (although much nicer, he thought secretly) who'd just been doing his duty. How brave to fly in those dangerous old planes to bomb the enemy. Albeson often turned his bed into the rear turret of a four-engined bomber and shot fighters out of the sky. What a rotten trick, when he was bound to be captured anyway, to try and kill him as he hung from his parachute.

Albeson never tired, either, of the tales of the prisoner of war camp, after grandad's leg had been cut off in a German hospital. Of the mad and daring escape plans, of the stupidity and brutality of the enemy. They talked about other things sometimes, but visiting hours in the old people's home were short, and the war had been so long and so full of excitement and danger and smashing daring deeds. Albeson preferred it when grandad had shared their home

23

with them, but he didn't get on with dad so that was that.
And the visits, short as they were, got fewer and farther
between however much Albeson urged his mum to take
him to the home. In fact he hadn't seen grandad for nearly
a month when he was told one day the fags had finally done
for the old devil (which was how his mother put it) and
they were to see him buried on Friday. His mum cried at
the funeral, which surprised Albeson a lot. He didn't cry,
but he remembered the funny leg and wondered if grandad's
body had it on in the coffin. And he missed the old man in
a way, and blamed it all on the Boche.

Later in the evening, waking with a start from a half
sleep, Albeson risked sneaking downstairs to nick some food.
He nearly had a heart-attack when Derek caught him
rooting about in the kitchen cupboard, but his brother just
cuffed him in a friendly manner and told him to make sure
there were no Germans – he called them Krauts – lurking
around to eat him.

'Not scared of Germans,' lied Albeson, his mouth full of
cheese, which was all his mother seemed to have in except
three eggs and half a cabbage.

'Not much you ain't,' Derek laughed. 'Like our Deena
eh? Hiding in Miss Gumley's office screaming her head
off. Nearly brought the place down they reckon, not that
you'd know, you skiving little arab. She's a disgrace to the
Albeson family if that was possible!'

'In her office? Crikey! What was she saying?' Albeson
bit off another bit of cheese, trying to make it look as though
it hadn't been touched.

Derek mimicked Deena's voice. ' "I'm scared of Germans
I am! I'm scared of Germans! I want to go home!" She's
right though, kidder, and don't you forget it! Them
Krauts'll eat you alive. Here, what you noshing?'

'Nothing,' said Albeson, heading for the door. 'Where's
mum and dad?'

'How should I know then? Down the bingo or the pub,
where d'you think? Mind the nightmares now.'

'What you on about, you ghost,' said Albeson, halfway through the door and dead daring.

'Nightmares. You been eating cheese, ain't you? Gives you terrible nightmares cheese does, last thing at night. You wait. They'll be there for you as soon as you drop off. Great big murderous monstery flesh-eating 'orrible 'airy Germans. Sweet dreams, kid. Ta ta!'

If Derek hadn't said it, maybe it wouldn't have happened. But he had. And it did. It had been a very tiring night, with grandad's lurid tales mixed up in a jumble with Smithie, Mrs Armstrong, his father, and the countless hordes from off the pages of his favourite comics, all shouting 'Achtung', 'English pigdog', 'Donner and Blitzen' and other peculiar oaths. Albeson had found himself time after time stuck on the barbed wire at the top of a prison camp fence as the machine guns opened up from the guard towers and the searchlights lit up the fangs of the dogs at the bottom waiting to tear him limb from limb. He paid even less attention to his lessons than he normally did, and at dinnertime Mrs Armstrong collared him as he tried to sneak out of the classroom.

'You look tired, Jimmy,' she said, smiling at him. 'Didn't you sleep well?'

Albeson shuffled his feet and hugged his lorry to him.

'Yes, Miss. All right.'

'What time did you go to bed? Late?'

That was a laugh. Albeson gave her a dazzling smile.

'About five o'clock, Miss!'

'Go on with you. What time really?'

'It's true, Miss. When I got home from . . .' He trailed off. He'd forgotten he'd played truant.

'Oh I see. Your dad sent you to bed did he? Very wise. You shouldn't do it, Jimmy. You need all the time in school you can get.'

'Yes, Miss. Sorry, Miss.'

Mrs Armstrong smiled to let him know she still liked him. Albeson didn't exactly know why, but she did like him, lots more than she liked any of the others. He liked her too, so that was all right, as long as she didn't nag him to do better at lessons and so on.

'How's your little sister today? Is she better?'

'Our Deena? Oh she's all right, Miss. She's a baby. Miss?' He really wanted to ask about the Germans, to be told they weren't coming after all, or that it would be all right. But he didn't know what to say.

'Yes, Jimmy?'

'Can I go now?'

She knew he wanted to ask something. She was very clever, Mrs Armstrong. She tapped him on the head.

'What do you think about Hans and Erica coming to the school, Jimmy? They'll be in our class you know. That'll be good, won't it?'

Albeson said nothing. He felt awful. Hans and Erica. They actually had names. They were real. And they were coming to his classroom. He felt terrible; frightened and silly. Why couldn't she understand?

'They start next Monday, isn't that nice? I bet you'll soon make friends with them, although we'll have to be extra nice because of course they don't speak a word of English. That's funny, isn't it?'

No no no no no, thought Albeson. It's not funny at all. She was going to let them in. She thought they'd all be friends. Hadn't Mrs Armstrong's grandad been in the war? Didn't she know anything about these terrible people?

'Your little sister seemed afraid. I don't know what she thinks Germans are. You'd have thought they had two heads each the way she went on. Said something about your grandfather having been in the war.' She paused. 'Jimmy. Are you listening? *Was* your grandpa in the war?'

Big-mouthed little fool, that Deena!

'Yes, Miss,' he said sulkily. 'He was in the Air Force. He was captured.'

To his surprise Mrs Armstrong laughed. He looked at her, shocked and angry.

26

'Oh well,' she said gaily. 'All that's over now of course. All water under the bridge as they say. We're friends now. Partners. All in the Common Market together. You've heard of the Common Market have you, Jimmy?'

He shook his head.

'Well I won't go into it now, but it means that England and Germany are the best of friends, the very best. Perhaps you'll tell Deena that, Jimmy, if she's still a little bit worried. Will you do that for me? Please?'

Albeson nodded and shuffled about a bit more. She patted his head again.

'You're a good boy, Jimmy. Sorry to keep you here in your dinner time. But I thought I'd better clear that little matter up. Make sure you tell her now, won't you? Afraid of Germans, the silly little thing! I'm glad we've got to the bottom of it. Run along now.'

Albeson ran. In the playground the kids were gathered in tight little bunches waiting for the dinner bell. They were talking about the Germans, and every one of them had a grandfather or an uncle or even a dad who'd been killed, captured or tortured in the war. They listened in awe as Albeson recounted some of the terrible things his grandad had suffered, until Billy Todd, who hated him, started calling him names, and saying the Albesons all ate rats, and his dad was a layabout. There would have been a fight, but the bell went so they had to go in to dinner.

Chapter 4

During the afternoon Mrs Armstrong talked to Albeson again, not about the Germans this time, but about his lorry. He was meant to be listening to the story, but he was miles away. It was a cloudy, muggy day and every now and again the smell of the sea, clean and cool over the stale chalky smell of the classroom, drifted in through the open windows. The school was a very old building with high ceilings and flint walls, and the windows were set well above Albeson's eye-level. He could just see a patch of sky, sometimes empty, sometimes filled with the flock of pigeons that were flying round and round the school, regular as clockwork. As he gazed out, his hand was stroking the cab of the Foden on his lap. In his head he was driving it up the M1, loaded with a cargo of gold and jewels, and the thieves behind him were getting closer and closer in their white Rolls Royce.

He didn't notice the tense silence that fell as Mrs Armstrong came towards him. He jumped as though he'd been shot when the lorry was plucked from his hands. Mrs Armstrong walked back to her table and sat down. She put the truck in her drawer.

'Perhaps you'd be good enough to pay attention now Jimmy,' she said. '*We* all think this is a very good story indeed. And after school I want you to tell me all about it.'

Albeson blushed and squirmed. He wondered how much

longer school would go on, and if he'd get his lorry back at the end of it.

When the others had finally gone, Albeson stood in front of Mrs Armstrong, trying to remember what the silly boring old story had been all about. But Mrs Armstrong did not ask him about it at all.

'Listen, Jimmy,' she said. 'You really must try to keep your mind on things. You've got a lot to learn. You know that, don't you?'

Albeson hung his head. He thought he'd go and see Pam in a minute. She'd know what to do about the Germans.

'Yes, Miss. Sorry, Miss.' He wondered if Pam was *really* a witch. She knew everything, and it was true her spells always came true. Could you be a witch and only thirteen years old?

The lorry was waved about in front of his face.

'This is a nice lorry. Have you had it long?'

Albeson stepped straight into the trap.

'Got it yesterday, Miss. Smi . . .' He bit his lip. Fool! 'It's a Foden, Miss. Real chains on the back see?'

'Smithie gave it to you did you say? Jimmy? Jimmy!'

He looked straight into her eyes and lied bravely.

'No, Miss. It was . . . it was our Derek. For my birthday. From his wages.'

Mrs Armstrong's big brown eyes held Albeson's grey ones until he looked at the ground. His toe was right out of his plimsoll now. It wasn't half dirty. He wiggled it.

'Jimmy, sometimes you are a very silly boy, do you know that?' He nodded, wiggling away. 'You know you are not allowed to play with that boy. You see . . . Well, it's not because . . . People aren't just being spoilsports you know, Jimmy. There are *reasons* for these things.'

'I won't again, Miss. Honest.'

'Did he buy it?' she said suddenly.

Albeson looked blank.

''Course he did,' he answered. 'From Woolies.'

'You're sure? He didn't . . . ?'

Albeson was fed up with all this.

'I won't play with him again, Miss. Honest I won't. He was waiting that's all, and you know how it is. I mean I couldn't run away could I? What could I do, Miss? I won't play with him no more.'

He flashed Mrs Armstrong his winning smile. The worried look on her face faded away and she smiled back. He grinned, showing all his teeth, and Mrs Armstrong laughed.

'Jimmy,' she said, 'you're a terror. I don't know what to say about you. Go on, run along. But, Jimmy – remember you promised. No more playing with Smithie.'

He turned the grin back into a nice smile and nodded. He liked Mrs Armstrong, she was a smasher. As he left she even called him back to give him the lorry he'd forgotten. He said thanks and meant it, then ran out. As he passed the paper shop Smithie darted out from behind the three-sided advert display that half-blocked the pavement. They went off to look for Pam together.

On the way to Hawthorn, where Pam lived with her mum and five brothers and sisters in the scruffiest house on the estate, Albeson listened to Smithie's tale of the fishing trip he'd been on all day with only half an ear. Smithie had caught a devil fish, which was interesting because if he'd touched it in the wrong place while getting it off the hook he'd have been dead in seconds. But while he was telling how he'd had to put it down a drain because he thought a policeman was going to search him – it was well known that it was against the law to carry such a dangerous fish about in a town – Albeson was wondering for the hundredth time exactly what everyone had against his friend.

He looked at him out of the corner of his eye as they strolled easily along through the busy, dusty streets. All right, so he dressed funny in his grey flannel trousers and his sports coat. But Smithie's Auntie Vi was bedridden and you couldn't expect Uncle Frank to know all about clothes could you? And he did look a bit peculiar with his bent sort of lop-sided face, but then he'd had that terrible accident when he'd been no more than Albeson's age, years ago. And his hair was wild and floppy and he tended to be dirty, not wash much. So what? Albeson's hair was short at the moment, but it was only the luck of the draw really. If his mum forgot to cut it for a month or two – which she often did – it'd be just like Smithie's. Albeson's brother Derek kept saying Smithie was a great big kid, and soft and all that. But he didn't know him, nobody did. He was tough, tougher than Derek, Albeson secretly thought, and he was smashing to play with, and had money, and knew great places to go like Flathouse, and the Camber, and fishing, and the pictures. Albeson had a twinge of regret about being with Smithie so soon after he'd promised Mrs Armstrong, but then grown-ups just didn't *know* about these things. Smithie was all right and that was that. And who else was there? The other kids were thick and soppy. That Billy Todd, saying Albeson's family ate rats. He'd do him tomorrow. He'd punch his rotten head in.

'Hey, nipper,' said Smithie. 'Ain't that Pammy over there? On the bomb-building?'

It was. They watched for a gap in the traffic and raced across the road, shouting. Pam looked up from the pile of oily engine bits she was arranging carefully on the scrubby grass of the bombed-site. She was squatting on her hunkers, with her dirty knees pointing outwards and oil everywhere. She grinned as they came panting up.

"Lo, Albeson. Wotcher, Smithie. What you at eh?"

'Hallo, Pammy,' said Albeson. 'We've been looking for you. What you doing?'

Pam's freckled face went serious. She pulled her hand across her forehead, through her straggly ginger hair.

'Found this stuff,' she said. 'I reckon there's been an accident. A big crash or something. I was just having a go at finding out.'

Albeson was amazed. She never stopped, Pam didn't. She knew all sorts of fantastic things and whenever you saw her she was up to something strange.

'Is it magic?' he said. 'Are you doing a spell?'

She tapped the side of her nose with her finger. 'Keep your cherry out, Albeson. Least said soonest mended, eh? Want to watch?'

Smithie flopped down on the ground in front of Pam, staring at her. Albeson knelt and looked at the pile of engine bits. There were three sparking plugs, a couple of small gear wheels, a ball-bearing race and a spring. Pam had arranged them in a pattern in the pool of oil and grease.

'How you going to do it?' asked Albeson.

Pam shifted position so that she was lying half on her side with her skinny legs stuck out of her long frock. She was the youngest in her family and she wore cast-offs, but Albeson liked the way she dressed. Everything was always a bit too big and it made her look like a sort of small grown-up. He studied every move as she started to stir the sticky liquid with a bit of metal pulled off an old pram.

'I'm going to mix up all this stuff with this here,' she said, pulling a little paint tin from out of her cardigan pocket. 'Can you open it up for me, Smithie?'

He did. It looked like red paint, very old and almost turned to glue. Pam got some on the end of her metal rod.

'What'll happen?' Albeson edged back a bit. He didn't want to be blown up.

'Well it depends,' said Pam. 'If I mix 'em up and they start to steam and smoke we'll have to wait. That'll mean there wasn't an accident and after a bit they'll just disappear. That *could* be it. On the other hand, if it sort of turns into a pinky mess and stays there – well, that's proof. There was a crash here and someone got killed.'

'Blimey,' said Smithie. He picked nervously at the red sore on his lip. 'You scared, nipper?'

'Nah,' said Albeson. He edged a bit further away.

'Righto then,' said Pam. 'Now, don't no one talk for a minute.'

32

As she touched the pool of oil with the bright red glob of stuff the sun went behind a cloud and the sky darkened abruptly. Albeson shivered and licked his lips. Smithie was tense too. Pam had her tongue clenched between her teeth, the pink tip of it sticking out of her mouth as she stirred up the gooey mess. When it was properly sticky she carefully planted the sparking plugs up in it like strange flowers. Then she closed her eyes and started muttering under her breath. The sun came out again, just as abruptly.

They all stared at the pinkish porridge for quite a long time. Nothing happened. No steam. No smoke. Smithie was beginning to fidget when Pam heaved a long sigh and sat happily back, legs out in front of her. She pulled up her brown sock and pinged the elastic.

'That's that then. There was definitely an accident on that spot. Just where you're sitting, Albeson, someone probably bled to death, groaning in agony.'

'Crikey,' said Smithie in deep awe. 'Ain't she clever, eh Albeson?'

Albeson shifted off the spot where he was sitting. He felt horrified. Someone's blood soaked into the grass. He wondered if the worms were still there, waiting for another lot.

'Don't worry, Albie,' Pam told him. 'I won't let anything hurt you. It was . . . oh, it was a couple of months ago I reckon, looking at the signs.'

She jumped to her feet and kicked the plugs, the spring, the gear wheels into a clump of long grass.

'What are we going to play then?'

Albeson swallowed. There was no doubt in his mind now. Pammy would tell him what to do about the Germans. It was a good move, coming to find her.

'No listen,' he said. 'Hang on a bit. I wanted to ask . . . Do you reckon you can . . . Well, listen.'

Pam and Smithie listened hard as he spilled out the story. Pam kept nodding her head from side to side and tutting with her tongue in a serious way. Smithie pulled his lip and scratched at his waistband. They both looked very worried. When he'd done, Albeson looked hard at Pam. She said nothing for a long time.

'Well,' he started at last. 'What shall I do? I mean . . . Well blimey, they eat human flesh.'

'That's right,' said Smithie. 'They killed my grandad they did. And they ate him too, I bet.'

It had never occurred to Albeson that Smithie had a grandad, being an orphan, but he was too anxious to hear what Pam would say to worry about it much. She was still deep in thought, shaking her head from side to side. At last she spoke.

'It's serious, Albeson. It's dead serious that is. We'll have to look in the crystal ball. Yes that is serious. *Very* serious.'

If it was a crystal ball job Albeson knew it was really bad, possibly a life and death matter. His mouth went dry. The crystal ball was in Fatty Hill's. And getting into Fatty Hill's was no easy business. He suddenly wished he hadn't told her. But it was too late.

'What *now*?' he said. 'Isn't it a bit late to get in? It must be tea-time I reckon.'

'Albeson,' said Pam in a deep voice, 'this is more important than tea. We've got to get into Fatty Hill's now. We've got to look in the crystal ball before it's too late. Smithie? Are you coming too?'

'You bet,' said Smithie. 'Let's hope Old Nobbler's having his tea too or we'll be in dead lumber.'

Important or not, Albeson was very relieved at what happened next. There was a loud shout of 'Pammy' from the other side of the bombed-site and Jean, one of her big sisters, appeared round a hoarding. Pam prepared to run but another shout, in a very nasty tone of voice, made her change her mind.

'Tomorrow morning,' she hissed. 'We'll go tomorrow morning.'

'But I've got school,' said Albeson, going pale.

'Who hasn't?' she replied. 'Meet me here about 9 o'clock.'

'I can't!' said Albeson, desperate.

'Albeson's yellow! Albeson's yellow!' chanted Smithie.

'It's *serious*!' Pam said. 'You've got to come.'

'I *can't*!'

'Don't worry, Pammy,' said Smithie. 'I'll bring him. See you outside the graveyard, nipper. Don't be late!'

He shouted the last bit, because Albeson was running. He had a horrible sinking feeling in his stomach.

35

Chapter 5

Any vague hopes Albeson had of giving Smithie the slip next morning were dashed as soon as he opened the front door. Instead of waiting at the cemetery he'd positioned himself exactly where Albeson had watched Mrs Armstrong from on Monday. He made sure Albeson had seen him, then ducked behind a bush in case any of the others did too. The clouds had gone in the night and it was a clear, sunny day. But as Albeson scuffed slowly over to his friend he felt far from cheerful. He didn't say much as they walked over to pick up Pam, who was waiting as promised. She looked as happy as a sandboy, with her face, hands and knees in exactly the state they'd been in the night before. Albeson marvelled at her dirtiness, and envied it too. His own mother wasn't too particular, but she did make sure he washed his face and hands before school.

As they got nearer Fatty Hill's his bad mood slowly wore off. It was, after all, a bit scary. And a rotten sight better than going to school, whatever he might have to suffer for it later. Fatty Hill's was a fantastic place to play in, although it was the most forbidden and the best guarded. You'd go to prison for sure if you were caught. With Old Nobbler on the prowl the chances of that happening were too high for comfort as well. This morning they weren't just going there to play, either. Pam was going to consult her crystal ball. After that the Germans would have no chance!

Fatty Hill's was a huge scrapyard, filled with rusty and

rotten metal of practically every type. It was surrounded by a high fence made of very old corrugated iron, with barbed wire on top in some places. On one side of the yard there was a great open space of spare ground where rows and rows of old terraced houses had been pulled down, and on the other were streets of boarded-up houses waiting for the bulldozers. The parts of the fence you could get over were on the spare ground side, so anyone who happened to be watching from the edge of the estate could see you. Old Nobbler lived in an old house stuck all on its own between the estate and the scrapyard. He was the watchman.

Albeson and Smithie, with Pam between them, wandered across the open space without saying a word. They felt as if every eye was watching them. The hair prickled on Albeson's neck and he was sweating, and not only because of the hot sunshine. When they reached the fence they walked along it as though they hadn't even noticed it was there, their eyes darting towards the estate in general and Old Nobbler's house in particular. At last they reached a spot where the corrugated iron had rusted right through. An old pram and a couple of crates had been pushed against the narrow hole from inside, but that was no problem.

'Here,' whispered Smithie. 'Stand in front of me while I push in this stuff.'

The noise he made kicking the barrier out of the way and tearing at the fence to make the hole bigger sounded incredibly loud. It seemed to go on for ages too. But just as Albeson thought he couldn't stand it any more there was a final tearing of metal and Smithie hissed: 'Come on. Get in quick!'

He followed Pam through the gap as though the hounds of hell were behind him. As soon as they were in they jammed the junk back against the fence so that no one would know they'd been through.

'Blimey,' said Pam. 'That's scary. And I've tore me dress.'

'Shut your row a minute and let's listen if there's anyone in here,' said Smithie.

They listened hard, but there was nothing to hear except the distant roar of traffic from the road. One good thing about Fatty Hill's was that the junk didn't get disturbed much. Whoever Mr Hill was – and he was just a name to them – he certainly didn't bother with his business that they ever noticed. Pam heaved a sigh of relief.

'Righto then, kids, let's go. This spell'll take a lot of doing I reckon. Let's get to the crystal ball.'

The junk was piled in separate mounds, with winding, rubbish-strewn paths between them. In one corner there were old engines, in another a huge assortment of washing machines, fridges and so on, and just along from them there was a small mountain of steel strips, old gas pipes, stair-rods and stuff like that. Smithie pointed this out to Albeson, not for the first time, as the place where Daniel Bullock had got killed.

'He climbed over the fence just there,' he said. 'Him and his mates was going to nick some of them rods to play sword fights with. He was just up at the top of the fence when Old Nobbler come along and set his dog on him. 'Course, his mates all run like mad, and Daniel Bullock was left up there like a blooming statue. Till he slipped, that is. Straight down he went like a stone. Stair-rod went right through him. Right through his front, right out his back. He died three days later.'

'I reckon that's murder,' said Pam. 'I reckon they should've hung Old Nobbler.'

'They don't hang 'em no more,' Smithie pointed out.

'Well they rotten well ought to that's all,' said Pam. Albeson agreed. Smithie had once showed him the stain where Daniel Bullock had fallen and bled. He always felt sick when he saw the pile of rods. He'd like to see Old Nobbler hang.

Smithie had been coming into Fatty Hill's for years now. He reckoned that once there'd been all war junk there. A real tank, with the machine guns still in it. You could get right into the turret and pretend you were driving it. He said there'd been guns as well, big ones on wheels, and American jeeps. Now the best things left were the old cars.

It was among the piles of cars that Pam had found her crystal ball. They'd been playing at gangsters, pretending to drive the wrecks, jumping from one to another, when they'd come upon a new one. Or new to the scrapyard at any rate, because they reckoned it was very old. It was big and flashy, obviously American, and Smithie said it must be a Cadillac. The bonnet had sprung open and pointed to the sky, and the engine compartment was so huge you could get into it. Pam had pulled a metal plate to one side and revealed a sort of half ball, of very shiny steel. If you breathed on it, then polished it up with your sleeve, weird patterns flickered across it like clouds across the sun. She'd discovered its magical powers there and then.

They picked their way to the smashed-up car section, gathering small twigs and bits of paper as they went. Pam had brought a box of matches to light a fire. This spell was going to be the real thing.

'Right,' she said when they'd settled down in the shade of the Cadillac. 'We've got enough wood. Smithie, you find a tin to make a pot with, Albeson you collect the deadly nightshade. I want twenty-seven berries, the black ones. No more, no less. And if you see any dandelions, bring nine. All right? It's important.'

Albeson wandered off towards the fence where the rough plants grew. He couldn't see any deadly nightshade at first, so he pushed cautiously through the junk, taking great care not to cut himself. Cut yourself on rusty metal and you got lockjaw, he knew. No cure; nothing could save you. You died in agony, your jaws shut tight, unable to eat, drink or talk – just groan.

Just beyond a stack of old tin cases he saw the berries. But as he climbed over a pile of wall bricks to reach them he spotted something else – a lizard, sunning itself on a piece of concrete. Albeson froze, then edged towards it, hardly breathing, moving a fraction of an inch at a time.

The lizard was brown and sleek, about three inches long. What a find! He hadn't caught one for ages. He reached out his hand very slowly, his tongue clenched between his teeth. Nearer, nearer, nearer. Then he lunged, making a hooked cup with his fingers.

In a flash of brown the lizard scuttled for a gap in the bricks. Albeson swore and closed his hand. He had it! No. Between his thumb and first finger the lizard's tail wiggled for a second or two, then was still.

He put the tail – which was better than nothing at all – into his trouser pocket while he gathered up the berries. Twenty-seven, no more no less.

Back at the car Pammy already had a little fire going and was pouring some bright pink liquid from a bottle into an old baked-bean tin balanced between two stones. Smithie was sitting on the running-board picking his lip.

'I didn't see any dandelions,' said Albeson, giving her the berries. 'But I nearly caught a lizard.'

'Cor, where?' said Smithie, jumping up.

'Over by the fence. But he's gone. Hid in a big pile of bricks.' He reached into his pocket and brought out the tail. 'Look at that though. He'll be sorry he ever went sun-bathing when I was about.'

They examined the bit of lizard with interest.

'Now *that*,' said Pam, 'is just the very thing. *That* will make absolutely rotten *sure* the spell works. Good old Albeson.'

Albeson blushed. Smithie looked a bit put out. Praise from Pammy was always welcome. He said: 'It'll die now, nipper, poor little thing. What harm did it ever do to you?'

'Won't die,' said Albeson. 'Crikey it's only its tail come off. Anyway I didn't do it. I didn't pull; it just came off in my hand.'

''Course it'll die,' said Smithie. 'Stands to reason. Won't it, Pam, eh?'

'I tell you what, Albie,' said Pam. 'As we're going to use his tail in the spell, I'll put in an extra drop of magic water and he'll be all right. He'll even grow another one. How will that suit?'

Albeson had heard long ago that if you pulled the tail off a lizard it grew another one, but he didn't argue. Pam had dropped him a big wink. Smithie might get a mood on him, which was the last thing they wanted.

'All right, Pammy,' he said. 'Thanks.'

Honour was satisfied.

When the pot was bubbling merrily Pam dropped the deadly nightshade berries in one by one. Then she sliced the lizard's tail up into tiny pieces with Smithie's Army knife. They went in too. After that they had to link hands round the pot, close their eyes, stick out their tongues, and walk slowly round and round in a circle. You could only move one foot at a time, bring it up to the next one till the ankles touched, then move that one till it touched your neighbour's ankle. Seven times to the left, seven times to the right.

'Now,' said Pam. 'You two go off for a bit. I've got special things to do that you mustn't see. Go over by the engines. I'll soon find you. We've got to leave it for a good long time.'

A few minutes later Pam joined them and announced everything was going well. They played several games of hide and seek, taking care to keep away from the Cadillac, then had a long session of cowboys and Indians. Finally Pam – who may have got fed up with being tied to a stake and burnt – said it was time to finish the magic.

When they got back to the car the fire was out and the purple brew in the tin had gone cold. Pam made Albeson and Smithie kneel down in front of the Cadillac's bonnet, that stuck up in the air like some sort of big beak. She dipped her finger in the potion and traced shapes on their foreheads. They had their eyes closed, but Albeson could feel Pam's breath on his face and neck as she muttered away, too quiet to make out the words. It was very still in the yard, just the low muttering and the distant rumble of traffic. Finally they had to sit cross-legged, eyes still shut, face to face with their knees touching. It was uncomfortable, because Smithie was so much bigger, but it never entered Albeson's head to argue with Pam. She'd been proved right too often.

He guessed from the clanking and banging that she was inside the engine compartment of the big car, consulting her crystal ball. Then she started speaking aloud, in a strange, ringing voice.

'Oh Albeson!' she chanted. 'It is indeed true that the Germans are coming! And it is indeed bad news, indeed.'

'Why?' Albeson panted.

'Shut up,' snapped Pam. 'You'll mess up the spell.'

There was silence for a long time. Then she went off again.

'Oh Albeson! There will come great trouble over these terrible eaters of men. There will be wailing and weeping and gnashing of teeth. I see in my crystal ball trouble, and a huge, giant dog, and a long journey, and fire and destruction.'

Another pause. Smithie was beginning to wriggle, from the effort of keeping his knees pressed down to meet Albeson's.

Pam chanted: 'I have consulted my oracle. I have asked the magic of the crystal. And she has said this . . .'

Albeson leaned forward. He felt giddy.

'She says you must take action to avoid disaster. She says you can stop them coming. But you will have to strike soon, and you will have to strike hard. She does not give details. Ah, here it comes . . .'

Another pause. Albeson was really aching now, really quite giddy. It was powerful magic.

'She says you, Jimmy Albeson, and you, Brian Smith, must enter Church Street School this weekend. She does not say what you must do, but I see fire and water, fire and water, fire and water.'

Albeson leapt to his feet.

'No,' he shouted. 'Mr Johnson said . . .'

'Albeson,' shrieked Pammy. 'Shut up! You'll ruin *everything*!'

But everything was ruined already. Round a pile of wrecked cars streaked a brown and white dog, barking frantically. It was followed a second later by a bent old man, red in the face with rage and waving a great knobbly stick.

'Over the fence,' shouted Smithie. 'Get over the fence! It's Nobbler!'

The old watchman must have been dead quiet as he crept up on them, but now he was shouting at the top of his cracked voice.

'You little villains! You little thieving devils! I'll tan your hides black and blue I will! You just wait till I catches you!'

'Fat chance of that, you old mug!' yelled Smithie. He jerked Albeson towards the fence and aimed a mighty kick at the little dog. But despite its furious noise it had more sense than to go too near the hefty boot.

They were all running now. Albeson felt a series of stabbing pains in his knees and hands as he clambered up an old bread van jammed against the rusty fence. It reached almost to the top. They could get over. Out of the corner of his eye he saw Pammy already hovering on the fence a few feet away. She was laughing at Old Nobbler. What a girl!

Old Nobbler lurched towards them. He was amazing when he ran. His legs were so bent that he rolled from side to side like a ship in a heavy sea. In his angry face his eyes glittered. He had on a bashed-about trilby hat and a heavy tweed jacket, despite the sunshine.

'You white-haired old dope,' Smithie shouted. 'You'll never catch us. You're too old!'

'Just you wait, young feller, that's all,' roared Old Nobbler. 'I know your names. I know who you are. I'll be round your school in a trice I will, you'll see. I've got your names, never you mind!'

He made a lunge at them and all three scrambled over the top. Albeson's jeans' pocket caught on the jagged metal and there was a loud tearing sound. As he fell and slithered to the open ground he left the pocket and a strip of trouser leg hanging from the fence. They could hear Old Nobbler hurrying round to a way out so that he could cut them off.

'Come on, nipper,' said Smithie. 'Run for it.'

Pammy was already halfway towards the estate, her long dress flapping around her knees.

'I can't! I've got to get that cloth! It's evidence!'

Smithie looked up uncertainly to the top of the fence. 'Come *on*! It's too high!'

'But he'll find it! The police!'

'Listen, if he catches you you'll go to jail anyway. Run!'

The dog, barking fit to bust with the excitement of it all, came haring round the corner of the fence. Smithie shot off, still yelling at Albeson to follow. Albeson didn't know what to do. He looked at the piece of cloth, then at Smithie, disappearing rapidly across the waste ground with the dog in full cry at his heels. Old Nobbler lurched into view, furiously waving the stick.

'I know you!' he panted. 'Just wait till I get me hands on you, you young ruffian! I know who you are!'

Albeson ran.

Chapter 6

To Albeson's horror, he had to miss school next day as well – and it was all his mother's fault.

After he'd run away from Old Nobbler, he'd drifted round the town in a sort of daze of panic. He knew he should have gone back to Fatty Hill's later to see if the cloth had been spotted by the old man and taken away for evidence. But he was sure it would have, anyway; Old Nobbler was not a fool. Then there was the chance that the police would already be there, lying in wait for him. What it boiled down to was that he was scared. He admitted it to himself, but it didn't make matters any easier.

At last Albeson had ended up in the Camber, which didn't surprise him because he always seemed to when he was just walking about, with nowhere definite to go. The *Carrie* still wasn't in but there was plenty to see and he forgot about his troubles after a while. The *Industrious*, a tough-looking little harbour tug that he liked almost as much as the *Carrie*, was towing a cluster of coal barges and he watched in awe as the captain and crew shuffled the huge unwieldy concrete things about as if they'd been plastic boats in a bath. A man was standing on the quay wall studying them as well, so Albeson was able to ask a question that had puzzled him for ages.

'Are them barges really made of concrete, Mister?'

'That's right, son. Cheaper than iron see?'

'Why don't they sink though? I mean, concrete doesn't

float does it? Stands to reason. If you chuck a bit of concrete in the sea . . .'

The bloke smiled at him. 'What about a lump of iron then eh? You reckon that would float if you dropped it in the 'Oggin?'

Albeson took the point and they chatted for quite a while. When the *Industrious* had finally sorted out the barges, one on each side and one on a short warp astern, and steamed slowly past Dirty Corner and out into the open harbour, the man bought him a bottle of lemonade and a packet of crisps. They sat on the wooden benches outside the 'Bridge', enjoying the sun and their 'liquid lunch' as his friend called the beer and pop.

He got home in time for it to look as if he'd been to school and found his mum in a smashing mood. The house was full of the smell of frying. It was fishfingers and chips, with lashings of tomato ketchup and bread and butter. Albeson made sure she didn't see the state of his jeans before he sat down, in case she banned him from his favourite meal. But she was cheerful and chatty anyway. So was his dad, who kept reading funny bits out of the paper to them.

'How d'you get on in school today then?' mum asked.

Albeson put down his tea-cup and looked cautiously at Deena. She was making a face on her plate with fish fingers for a mouth and chewed-up potato for eyes. He'd cornered her in the street before she'd got home from school anyway. She wouldn't dare split on him.

'Smashing,' he said, and filled his mouth with chips to avoid answering any more questions.

'That's nice,' said his mum. 'I hope you learned a lot, Jimmy, because you've got to stay away tomorrow.'

He swallowed too quickly, which made him cough. His eyes watered as he fought to get his breath back. Derek thumped him, not too gently, on the back.

'What do you mean?' he said at last. 'Can't miss school. I'll get told off!'

'I'll give you a note, silly,' said mum. 'Come on, Jim,

46

you'll enjoy it. Me and dad have got to go out for the day and the rent man's due. And the gas.'

Albeson was put right off his food. What with all these days off, then Pam's spell. He'd be in dead trouble. He would for sure. He tried again.

'It's not rotten fair! I was off on Monday. I was warned. I'll get the cane or something. She'll send me to Mr Johnson.' Mr Johnson was headmaster of the juniors; Deena's mouth opened in shocked delight. Albeson hated her. He wanted to pull her hair. His dad put down his paper.

'Whose fault is it you were off on Monday eh? You played truant. If you get caned you deserve it. Too fond of pleasing yourself by half you are. Now shut up. I'll have no more argument.' He poked his nose back in the paper. Albeson was nearly crying.

'Come on, Jimmy,' said his mother. 'We've got to go and see about a new place to live. Along the coast. Your daddy'll get a new sort of job and we'll have a big new house. He's fed up with the Dockyard. We're going to live in the country.'

Derek started whistling under his breath. The tune was 'That'll be the day'. It stopped suddenly as the paper came down again and dad stared at him. Albeson felt very unhappy. It was less than six months since his father had decided to move the last time. It happened quite a lot and it always seemed to cause a lot of trouble. But they still lived on Briar. Albeson had been born there.

'I can't, mum,' he muttered. 'I'll get into trouble.' But he said it so low that he could hardly be heard.

'The rent man will be here in the morning, and the gas man said about dinner time. Then the Provident man'll most likely be here about three or four o'clock. The football pools man might turn up too, you never know. I'll leave all the money in separate envelopes on the mantelpiece. You see, Jimmy, there's lots coming. There's got to be somebody here. Do you want some more chips?'

Deena said: 'Ooh yes, mum! More for me! More for me!'

'Shut up, you. Jimmy? Do you want more chips?'

Albeson shook his head. Derek laughed at him.

'I know what's up with him,' he said. 'After next week he won't be able to go to school in case a flipping German eats him. So he wants to learn everything by the weekend!'

Deena started to wail, but mum quickly ladled the spare chips on to her plate and she subsided with her mouth full. Albeson stood up.

'Where *did* you do that, you bad boy!' said his mother. 'Jimmy, your bum's sticking out of your trousers!'

Everyone roared with laughter then, even Albeson. He was glad to get off with it so lightly – normally he'd have been cuffed a few times at the very least. But the prospect of a day out, and no doubt a few drinks into the bargain, had made his mum act like a kid herself. After tea, when Albeson was watching television, she got a piece of spare material and patched up his jeans. It was red, but that didn't worry anyone. Despite his worries Albeson, tired and full of chips and bread, fell asleep as soon as he got into bed.

Quite early in the morning he had the house to himself. There was a meat pie in a cellophane wrapper on the kitchen table for his dinner, beside a small bottle of lemonade his mother must have got from the pub. There had been a packet of cheese and onion crisps as well, but Albeson had scoffed them almost before his mum and dad had reached the bus stop at the bottom of the street. By half-past-ten he was fed up with sailing a submarine-shaped piece of wood in the sink, and fed up with driving his Foden round the kitchen floor. He wasn't allowed to go out. There was nothing at all to do.

At about eleven-thirty the rent man had gone and so had his dinner. He went up to his parents' bedroom, watching Briar's quiet workday life crawling past. He jumped up and

48

down on the bed for a bit, but the springs were old, or bust, so it didn't bounce much. After the gas man had been and gone Albeson went to his own bed and lay down. He cried for a while, then went off into a doze.

He dreamed awful dreams of policemen and Old Nobbler and the little brown and white dog with enormous fangs chasing him round and round Fatty Hill's taking chunks out of his legs. He answered the door to streams of men in black hoods who matched up the torn cloth of his jeans with the scarlet patch. He woke up sweating and cried some more. He was bored and very very lonely.

Albeson was quite sure something bad would happen to him now he'd missed his third day in one week, note or no note. Mrs Armstrong liked him, tried to be nice to him, but she couldn't just let him get away with this sort of thing. It just wasn't on. The next day he'd be hauled up before Johnson as sure as fate. The caning would be the easiest part to bear. But old Johnson would insist on seeing his dad, or sending the attendance man round or something. Albeson's dad was a difficult man for such people to get on with. There'd be trouble, a fight or a row or something terrible. Then when it was all over his dad would take it out on him. With his belt — buckle down.

And as if all that wasn't bad enough, what about the rest? Pam said he and Smithie had to go into the school to stop the Germans coming. Albeson knew rotten well what he'd rather do — let them come. Maybe they did eat people. Maybe there would be awful fights. Maybe it would be like the war all over again. But he'd rather do anything than break into the school.

He hadn't done it, been in at a weekend, for a long time now. Once he and Smithie had made a regular thing of it, it was sort of a Saturday treat like going to the picture club only better (and cheaper). They didn't do much that could be considered very bad, just ate the biscuits in the nursery class, drew rude pictures on the blackboards, chucked books about and pulled pictures off the wall, that kind of stuff.

Once they'd taken some money – a few pence – they'd found in one of the teachers' coats that must have been forgotten. Albeson had worried about that a lot. He wouldn't look in pockets or desks from then on, but no one had ever said anything special about it.

The break-ins had stopped abruptly after Mr Johnson had given the whole school a terrible speech about it one Monday morning. He said the school had been entered that weekend (which it had, by Albeson and Smithie) and that the police were even now making inquiries. He expected the culprits to be unmasked at any moment, as they had been making a habit of it and had left hundreds of clues. In any case, he said, woe betide anyone who had done it in the past or who might be foolish enough to do it in the future.

Even with this frightful warning fresh in his mind Albeson had found it hard to persuade Smithie they had to stop doing it. He'd called him yellow, and a spoilsport, and threatened to punch him up. But Albeson had been determined, even when Smithie made him cry. There had been no arrests as week after week went by, but they got used to not going in. It had faded from their minds.

The trouble with Smithie was this: Albeson might dare to defy Pam over the spell, but it would never enter Smithie's head. He'd jump at the excuse to break into the school again, and it was a pound to a penny that he'd force Albeson to as well, whether he wanted to or not. There was no way of getting round Smithie when he'd decided on something; he'd wait till he caught Albeson, drag him along, then they'd be tracked down by the police, probably using dogs. He didn't fancy the idea of going to prison one little bit but that was that.

It was after four when the next knock came at the front door; Albeson knew because he had to lift the alarm clock off the living room mantelpiece to get to the last two money envelopes and he noticed the time. It would be the Provident man he guessed. The football man usually came much later. He picked up the envelope his mother had marked with a big P (the other had a football drawn on it) and went to the front door.

'Hello, Jimmy,' said Mrs Armstrong. 'I came to see if anything was wrong.'

Chapter 7

Albeson felt a complete fool. He suddenly realized his face must be all tear-stained and dirty. There he was, with his mouth open and the Provident money clutched in his hand, facing the last person in the world he wanted to see. He'd forgotten all about school, because Deena hadn't come home. She'd been told to go to Auntie Mary's for her tea. He gulped.

Mrs Armstrong smiled at him.

'Is there anything wrong, dear? Are your mummy and daddy in?'

Albeson thought of the note mum had said she would write.

'I'm not very well,' he muttered. 'Mum said I had to stay off school.'

'Oh dear,' said Mrs Armstrong. 'What's wrong with you, Jimmy?'

He was stumped. He slowly went bright red. He felt the heat go up his neck into his cheeks and then his ears. They burned.

A man appeared behind the teacher.

'Hello, sonny,' he said. 'Provident. Is your ma in?'

Albeson looked at the ground, holding out the envelope marked 'P' dumbly in front of him. The man took it and wrote in a notebook.

'Gone out for the day has she, nipper? Ah well, thanks a lot. Cheerio!'

Mrs Armstrong touched his arm.

'Can I come in for a minute, Jimmy? I want to talk to you.'

In the sitting-room Albeson sat on the sofa. He had his lorry on his knees, although he hardly noticed it. He felt very much like crying again. Mrs Armstrong moved some papers off a chair and sat down. He didn't look at her.

'Jimmy,' she said after a while, 'you've not been to school three days this week. You'll be getting into hot water before long, don't you know that? Jimmy, try and concentrate on what I'm saying, don't play with your lorry, dear.'

He shrugged his shoulders. He wasn't playing with it. He stared at his knees. Mrs Armstrong tried again.

'So far nothing terrible's happened, Jimmy, but if you go on playing truant something will have to be done. The headmaster will get to hear of it, then the attendance officer. It will all be very uncomfortable. You don't want that now, do you?'

Albeson shook his head, but he did not look up.

'What I really want to know, Jimmy, is if there's a special reason. I know you're not very fond of school, and that sometimes the other children rag you. But they don't mean anything by it you know. Children often say unkind things, but no harm's meant. I expect you do it yourself sometimes. We all do when we're young.'

Oh yeah, he thought. He bet no one ever said Mrs Armstrong's family ate rats when she was a little girl. He bet her dad wasn't a dockie who all the kids said spent more time thinking about it than going out to work.

'You see, what puzzles me is why you've started staying away like this. Well everyone has the odd day off we all know that. Even teachers have been known to say they're ill when it's not strictly true. But your record is really quite good, Jimmy, and I think there's a reason. I think there's a *sudden* reason. Something's happened to make you worried and that's why you're truanting. And I think I know what it is.'

Albeson went cold. Had he been found out already? If Mrs Armstrong knew about Fatty Hill's she must have been told by the police. Or if they hadn't told her, it stood to reason she'd tell *them*: that was the way grown-ups worked. She must also know he'd been playing with Smithie again, after he'd promised not to. Crikey, he'd be in trouble! He glanced up at Mrs Armstrong and she smiled. Albeson stared down again, his hands clenched hard around the lorry.

'It's the Germans isn't it? You've got some funny idea in your head about the Germans? Well I've got a plan, Jimmy. I want you to listen to it very carefully and tell me what you think. Well dear, am I right? And will you listen?'

Albeson was much too confused, and uncomfortable, and downright scared, to sort out exactly what he did feel about anything just at that moment. He nodded his head a few times, and made a funny noise in his throat. Mrs Armstrong obviously took it as a sign that she was right and that he would listen. Her voice got quite jolly.

'I knew I was right. Oh you are a funny boy, Jimmy! You're a dream! No I'm not laughing at you. I think it's perfectly natural, really, what with all the films they have on telly, and the comics and everything. Even if you believed that Germans ate human flesh – and people used to you know! – you could be forgiven. But of course it's all total nonsense. Total.'

Total nonsense. Fat lot she knew. A vision of the lizard's tail slowly bubbling up and down in the purple brew came into Albeson's head. Go into the school, said Pam, go into the school and you will stop them coming. Fire and water and a dirty great dog. Fat lot she knew.

'Listen, I'll tell you about the family, about Hans and Erica's daddy and mummy. Their father is an engineer and he's come over here because he can help out the English people with some special things he knows – he's very very clever. But it's not the first time he's been here, Jimmy. He's quite young – thirty-five I think, and that's quite young believe me, although you might not think so now.

54

But although he's only young, he's actually lived in England before, for a long time. In fact, you could almost say he's more English than German. There, what do you think of that?'

Albeson looked at Mrs Armstrong. He opened his mouth, showing willing, but couldn't honestly think of anything to say. But he was interested. Perhaps he wasn't a German after all. But he was! You couldn't be 'almost', whatever she said. Mrs Armstrong flashed him a smile and he tried to show her one back. It didn't work out very well, but it was something.

'Good,' said Mrs Armstrong. 'Feeling better are we, Jim? Now listen. Mr Grundmann really is *very* English. He even speaks English with a northern accent, because he lived in Manchester for a long time. His daddy was an engineer too, and he came to England to work when Mr Grundmann was a little boy about as old as you. That was a long time ago, more than twenty years. But he stayed there, and grew up there, and went to school in Manchester like any other little boy. When he went back to live in Germany – that was about 1960 I think – he practically had to learn to speak the language again. Isn't that funny!'

'What did *his* dad do in the war?' said Albeson.

Mrs Armstrong looked a bit flustered.

'Oh Jimmy! We're not talking about his father. We're talking about Mr Grundmann.'

'Yes,' said Albeson stubbornly. 'But what *did* he do? My grandad says the Boche –'

'We don't call them that, dear,' said Mrs Armstrong in her schoolteacher voice. 'We don't call people names.'

Albeson was surprised. He didn't know it was calling names. He'd never thought of it. Mrs Armstrong was sailing on.

'When Mr Grundmann went back to Germany and when he could speak the language well again he met a nice German lady and they got married, of course. And had two children, as you know. But Mr Grundmann always wanted to come back. He loves this country. He says he'd like his children to grow up like British children. He even likes our climate, Jimmy! The weather.'

'Did his dad fight in the war? He might have shot down my grandad. One of them shot down his plane then tried to kill him on his parachute. He was a rear gunner. They cut his leg off.'

He didn't look at Mrs Armstrong as he said this. He knew he should have kept his mouth shut but he didn't care. The alarm clock ticked loudly on the mantelpiece. There was quite a long pause.

At last she said: 'Jimmy, I understand. Believe me I *do* understand. You must have loved your grandad and wars are . . . Well believe me, Jimmy, there are just some things that you can't know about. When you're older you'll see. Please believe me. You do trust me, Jimmy, don't you?'

He nodded without interest. What else did she expect him to do? Grown-ups were a puzzle, but not one to get excited about. How could she sit there and expect him to believe her when she couldn't deny that this rotten German's rotten dad might have blown off grandad's leg? He remembered grandad vividly for a moment; short and scruffy, stinking of fag smoke, his leg hard and amazing to Albeson's knuckles. Tap-tap. He missed him, just for a second.

Mrs Armstrong didn't sound so jolly when she spoke again. 'It's very difficult to explain, it truly is. But it was a long time ago now, Jimmy. All that's past. We don't think or mind about all those terrible things that happened once. I told you before and it really is true – our two countries are the best of friends. Mr Grundmann's more English than an Englishman in some ways, and he wants his little boy to grow up just like an English boy – just like you, for example.'

Playing truant and chucking stones through windows and trying to get on buses without paying. Oh yeah. Albeson was bored. He wished she'd go away. Perhaps the football man would come.

'Anyway, Jimmy, I'll tell you my plan. It's going to be smashing fun. And you'll find out for yourself then. You'll know that everything I've been telling you is the honest truth. Straight from the horse's mouth.'

That expression, 'straight from the horse's mouth,' an expression his mother used over and over again, opened up a huge empty pit in Albeson's stomach. What was she going to say? What was he going to hear 'straight from the horse's mouth'?

'You see, Hans and Erica's daddy is a bit worried about them. Neither of them can speak any English at all, and he's worried that they won't make any friends. They're living in that big old stone house along Albert Road, do you know it? It *is* a bit far away from the school, although of course he'll take them in by car every day and pick them up again. But it's not very near where the other children live, is it? So Mr Grundmann asked me if I knew any children I thought might like to go to tea at the house. Just once or twice, you know, so that they could get to know each other. Make friends.'

She paused, looking at Albeson. The pit in his stomach had become bottomless. He *wouldn't* meet the Germans. He *wouldn't* meet the Germans!

'Well naturally, Jimmy, I thought of you at once. I know you've got this funny thing, this sort of fear of them. And I'm quite sure, I'm absolutely certain, that if you met Hans and . . .'

'No!' Albeson stood up wildly. His lorry went spinning off his knees onto the floor.

Mrs Armstrong looked startled. She bent down and picked up the lorry.

'Now, Jimmy, you haven't heard it all yet. Don't be a silly boy, I think I know what's best. Now listen, dear, if I were to arrange with Mr Grundmann that you went to tea. Jimmy . . . ?'

Albeson had heard a key in the front door.

'You've got to go now, Miss, you've got to go.'

'But what do you think, Jimmy? Hans and Erica would love . . .'

Albeson almost fainted with panic as the sitting-room door opened. His mother came in. She was looking flushed, sort of untidy and hot and cross. She jumped when she saw Mrs Armstrong.

'Oh hello, Mrs Albeson,' said Mrs Armstrong cheerfully. 'I just came round to ask Jimmy . . .'

'He's been ill,' said Mrs Albeson. 'He would've had a note for the morning and that's that.'

'But you don't understand.'

Albeson felt his dad come into the room. He just knew from the feeling on the back of his neck that his dad had walked through the door.

'Look who's here,' said his mum in a funny voice. 'Jimmy's teacher come to check up on us. That's nice isn't it?'

Mrs Armstrong went very red, then started to go white.

'You don't understand,' she said. Her voice was funny too, sort of cracked and high. 'I just . . .'

'Well you can just get out. Just get to the door and get out!' Thick, Albeson's dad's voice was, like treacle, but quivering. Albeson was shaking. His father had been drinking, they both had. That's why mum looked hot and vicious.

'I wanted to ask if Jimmy . . .'

'You can't ask nothing,' said his mum. 'You've no right to come in here without permission. This is my house. You've no right!'

'If the little sod needs a whipping he'll get it,' said his dad. 'It's nothing to do with you. And it's none of your business if we keep him at home or not the odd day. Just don't come round here snooping, got it?'

Through his tears Albeson saw Mrs Armstrong nod. Her blurred form came up to him and handed him the lorry. He dropped onto his knees and started to sob. Oh *why* couldn't she leave him alone? But she was still thrusting it at him. The lorry, the lorry. At last his father realized.

'Whose is that truck? Are you giving my boy presents

now? You'll get what's coming to you if you're not careful!'

Her voice came through his sobs, loud and clear. 'Mr Albeson I did not give that child anything. He tells me – well never mind. No, I will say it. That boy is intelligent, funny and hopeful and I can't bear to see . . . Mr Albeson, he is playing truant and he is being led into deep water. If you don't know who by, then I suggest you find out.'

Albeson gave a howl then. He threw himself onto his face in a squall of sobs. She'd betrayed him. He cried, crumpled into a heap on the edge of the fireplace, waiting for the storm to break. He didn't see or hear the going of Mrs Armstrong, he didn't know if the row finished or carried on. When his father jerked him upright by his arm and belted him hard across the face he wasn't sure if it was a few minutes later or the middle of next week. He didn't listen to what his father said, and after a while he didn't feel the blows or the cutting edge of the belt buckle. It was a storm, a wild, horrible, ringing, headlong storm.

Much later he woke up. He was lying on his bed with swollen face and eyes, fully dressed. There were aches and pains galore but it was too dark to see anything. There was something hard pressing into his side. He fumbled for it, pulled it up to his face. The Foden flat truck. It had been smashed up with a hammer.

Chapter 8

Classrooms, when they were quiet and empty, were very odd places. Albeson never noticed that school had a special smell during the week, but now, on Saturday afternoon, as he crouched behind the tall desk in the hall where they said prayers, he kept taking in big breaths through his nose, snuffing the odd mixture that seemed to be part chalk, part damp anoraks, part children. He sniffed at his hand: nothing. Then he raised his head again and breathed in the smell. He didn't like it.

Smithie came through the hall door carrying the biscuit tin from the nursery.

'What you doing hiding behind there for, you ghost?' he said when he spotted Albeson. 'Nobody can see you in this old dump. The windows are too high.'

It was true. The school could have been built for giants. The window sills were way above Albeson's head, and even Smithie had to stretch just to touch them. Silly, having windows you couldn't see out of. He asked Smithie why they'd made them that way.

'Dunno really, nipper. Maybe they thought if all the kids could see out no one would listen to the boring old teachers. Dead right too I shouldn't wonder. Anyway,' he added, 'makes it difficult for thieves too, don't it? I mean them high windows, you'd need a ladder to break in!'

He laughed at his own joke, because as usual he and Albeson had found it about as easy to break into Church

Street as it would have been to get in if the doors were open. They'd gone round the back of the boiler house, onto the wall of the babies' lavatories, up the annexe roof to the open skylight, and down. It was a five foot drop or so for Smithie, then he'd pushed a table underneath for Albeson to land on. They couldn't get out the same way, but that was even easier. There were so many doors in the old place, not to mention the floor-level windows in the annexe. One of them was always ready to come open if you pushed hard enough from inside, or in emergencies you just broke the glass. Like so many other parts of town, the school was isolated in a mass of boarded up or falling down houses. Not much chance of being spotted outside, let alone in. And the caretaker, Mr Kowalski, spent practically every hour he wasn't at work on his allotment.

Albeson left the shelter of the desk and joined Smithie in a classroom. It was nice and sunny, and they ate the biscuits with a bottle of pop Smithie had bought – lime cream soda, their favourite taste.

'You scared any more, Albeson?' asked Smithie. Little sprays of chocolate biscuit showered from his mouth as he spoke.

'Nah,' said Albeson. 'Never was, was I?'

'Don't give me that! You didn't want to come! Giving me all that tripe about a bad stomach and that, must think I was born yesterday. What'd Pammy say if we didn't go in eh? And what about them Krauts! They'd've ate you Monday. Now they're in dead lumber.'

Albeson munched at a biscuit thoughtfully. It was true he'd tried to put Smithie off. He'd even tried to do it by not leaving the house, knowing that he'd never have dared knock and ask for him. But his mother wouldn't wear that. When the sun was out, so was Albeson. She didn't want him under her feet. Outside he'd spotted Smithie at once, in the usual place behind the bush. He'd made a couple of excuses, but only for the sake of it. Short of trying to run away altogether, or getting his neck broken or something, he had to go into school. No point in arguing the toss.

But he had been scared, terrified. Talk about 'between the devil and the deep blue sea!' He hadn't heard what dad had said to him during Thursday's beating, but he knew what it was about. It was about a boozy day out that had gone wrong (he'd got no job, Derek had said next day; surprise surprise!) but it was about other things too. Mrs Armstrong calling, the lorry, Smithie. Mrs Armstrong had told dad about Smithie, Smithie had given him the lorry, dad had belted him. Now here he was, only two rotten days later, breaking into school with him. What a mess-up. The Germans coming, the attendance officer on the prowl, the police catching them over this or Fatty Hill's, his dad belting him over Smithie, and Smithie quite capable of filling him in if he tried to get out of it all. As they'd wandered through the buzzing, heat-filled streets Albeson had been almost dizzy with terror. What a fantastic mess!

In school on Friday nothing had been said about Mrs Armstrong's visit. She didn't talk to Albeson as much as normal, but that was hardly surprising because he did his best to keep out of her way and keep his mouth shut. He had a bruised eye but it didn't show all that much. For the rest, well his jeans and shirt looked the same as ever, whatever state he might have been in under them. Towards the end of the afternoon she came up and he thought she was going to say something about it, but Albeson felt a blush climb into his cheeks. He could have sworn she went red too. She turned round and started looking for something in her drawer.

Now, listening to the glugging sounds as his adam's apple bobbed up and down on a stream of pop, he was quite happy in a way. He put down the bottle and took the last chocolate biscuit.

''Course I wasn't scared,' he said. 'I'm not scared of no Germans and I'm not scared of this lot. Eh Smithie, it's fun this, isn't it? Just like old times!'

'You've hit the nail on the head, nipper. We ought to start

this up again like we used to, Germans or no Germans. Haven't had as many biscuits as this for I don't know how long.'

'Lucky little pigs, the babies. Our Miss don't give us anything like this. Excuses excuses! She says sweets and biscuits are bad for our teeth.'

'Dah,' said Smithie. 'You can always get false ones!'

When the tin was empty Smithie turned it upside down and jumped on it. Albeson took the lid over to the wall, using the corner of it to tear the paintings and silly pictures across. There was a farmyard scene, felt animals, green trees, fat farmers, a tractor and some pigs. It was on soft felt sheet, pretty big, with all the rest stuck on, made out of bright coloured material. Albeson started in a small way, pulling off a leg here, a head there. Then he picked up the box-lid, ripping and tearing the point through the whole picture. It looked funny, hanging down from the wall in tatters. He could imagine the little kids when they saw it on Monday. Crikey, that would get 'em crying!

In the room next door he found Smithie collecting all the coloured chalks into a big heap on the floor. It was the music and dance room, where you had to learn country dancing. The floor was pale and polished.

'Get the chalks, nipper. Go round all the classes, hurry up! All the coloured chalks in the school!'

Albeson got the idea. They'd pile them up in a big pile, then crush them. They'd jump up and down on them and grind them up and smear and spread them into the pale, shiny floor. Yeah, that was really something. That would show them what the kids thought of their soppy dances. Albeson had been in love with a girl called Jean Rouse some time before, and for a short time he'd done country dancing at every possible chance, just for the thrill of touching her as they swapped partners. But she'd gone to Australia to live, and anyway she didn't love him. He ground a piece of red chalk underfoot as an experiment. It looked fine. When he walked off he left a foot-shaped splodge. It was terrific!

Half an hour later the floor had disappeared under a thick, dusty layer of the most amazing colours. It was mainly red, with great streaks of blue and yellow. In one corner there was a wide patch of lurid green, where they'd found a new box of crayons in a drawer. They skated round in the mess, tracing patterns with their feet. Smithie had taken his jacket off. There were big patches of wet under his armpits, making his thick grey shirt black. His face was bright and smiling, his hair wild. In the excitement his lop-sided smile seemed much more obvious than usual. He kept giving whoops of delight, but Albeson shushed him. They might not be able to be seen in the school, but it wouldn't do to make too much noise.

'Hang about a sec, nipper,' Smithie said as they danced a pretend country dance in the mess. He raced out of the class and there were loud bangs nearby. As he came back there was a smash close to Albeson and liquid sprayed over the table, nearly catching him. Smithie had broken into the ink store. He lifted another litre bottle ready to chuck.

'Look out, look out!' Albeson hissed. 'Don't get it on me, you nutcase! It's evidence! It's evidence!'

Smithie lowered the bottle.

'All right, Albeson, don't wet yourself. Come over here if you don't like it.'

Albeson joined him at the door and looked in. What a sight! He said to Smithie. 'I know, we ought to do one of them things – you know, them German things. The cross.'

'Swass-something,' said Smithie. 'Swasstick or something. Yeah, that's it. How do you do it now?'

Albeson unscrewed the litre of blue-black ink. He walked carefully across the floor, first of all making an ordinary cross, very big, about six feet each direction. Then he poured out the extra bits, not very well, so that there was a great crooked blue-black Swastika in the gaudy mess of chalk. They looked at it in awe.

'Now they'll know it's something to do with the Germans,'

said Albeson. 'Pammy should just see that now! She'd reckon we've done a real job!'

'Yeah, she should've been here, the chicken!'

'Chicken? Don't be daft,' said Albeson. 'It was the spell. She knows the magic. You can't go against it.'

'Magic nothing,' said Smithie. 'She's yellow she is. She sends us in here to do it and if anyone gets caught that's their look-out. She's never been in, Pam ain't, and we've offered enough times.'

From this point on Albeson felt the fear creeping back. He would have gone on arguing but Smithie had other things to think about. He grabbed the bottle from Albeson. It was still half full and Smithie held it like a bomb. He turned into the hall and lobbed it high into the air, up into the funny cream-painted beams in the high, church-like roof. It rose over a beam, then spun down, spraying ink everywhere, till it smashed into the end wall above the platform. A huge stain spread over the big blackboard and the school motto. He gave another whoop, even louder than before. Albeson said 'Ssh' and Smithie turned on him and snarled 'Shut up!'

Then Smithie gripped Albeson's wrist and ran across the hall, jerking him along like a parcel. At the store cupboard he took the last two litres of ink, unscrewing the caps and chucking them away.

'German crosses everywhere,' he said. 'Where's your classroom? We'll do one in there.'

Albeson ran about with his friend, spreading ink, knocking over tables, making a mess, but he wasn't enjoying it any more. Smithie was making more and more noise, was breaking things more and more wildly. Albeson wanted to tell him to stop, wanted to stop him shouting, wanted to shout *at* him, to scream at him to give it up and run, run, get out of there. But he didn't dare. Smithie was red with excitement, dripping with sweat, stinking with sweat. His face was tense and quivering, his mouth was quite bent, all to one side. He was dribbling a little, too, from the lop-sided corner of his mouth. And he kept shouting, kept letting out great whoops that rang through the empty school and filled Albeson with terror.

By the time they got to Mrs Armstrong's room, where the Germans were actually to be taught, there was no more ink to make Swastikas with. Smithie seized the chalk from the blackboard ledge and scrawled them on the board. He told Albeson to tear down the pictures, but Albeson was tired now. He was tireder than he'd ever been, it seemed to him. He sat down at his table, in his special chair, and watched Smithie.

He made an incredible mess in a very short time, and though he kept shouting for Albeson to join in, he didn't force him. Finally he stopped by the fish tank. He was panting, with sweat actually running off his forehead and nose onto his shirt, which was by now almost completely black.

'Fishes,' he said. 'It's rotten fishes, Albeson!'

'Yeah,' said Albeson. 'Miss keeps 'em. She likes 'em. Says they're beautiful to look at. All sorts there are. You keep 'em warm with an electric thing.'

'What, this?' said Smithie. He jerked the wire and the glass heater leaped out of the fish-tank onto the floor. He put the heel of his shoe on it and pressed. Crunch.

'They'll die now, you ghost,' said Albeson. 'She'll go hairless.' He was too tired to be afraid, or angry; or anything in fact.

'Oh, poor little things,' said Smithie. He pointed to a tube that was blowing bubbles into a corner of the tank. 'What's that then?'

'Dunno,' said Albeson. 'Oxygen or something I think. Leave it be, Smithie. We'll get into awful trouble.'

Smithie jerked and pulled at the tube, grunting. Inside the tank the small, bright fishes flashed about at great speed, terrified Albeson supposed. The tube came away and the bubbles stopped.

'Poor little fishikins,' said Smithie. 'If they don't freeze, they'll choke to death! Might as well put 'em out of their misery, eh nipper?'

It felt as though Albeson was holding up a great weight as he watched Smithie smash up the fish tank. First he tried with a kid's chair, but it broke. Then he just leaned back, swung his leg far behind him, and went through the glass with one kick. A gush of water shot across the floor all around Albeson's feet. As it sank into the boards it left the poor bright fish flapping feebly in the dirt.

Albeson gasped for breath. It was as though he was drowning too. He wasn't tired any more. He wanted to open his throat and scream and howl. He was drenched with fear. Smithie stood in the middle of the room, his face still, his lip twitching, soaked from the knees downwards. Bits of weed were stuck all over his trousers, gravel from the shattered tank was in a little pile on the toe of his shoe. The water near his feet was stained red, the stain spreading wider and wider as blood from his cuts ran down inside his trouser leg, into his shoe, and over the edge to the floor.

They were both white and shaking as they crept out of the school into the hot, still city.

Chapter 9

Going to school on Monday morning was the worst thing Albeson could remember in his life. Over the whole weekend he hadn't been able to keep out of his mind what he and Smithie had done. It was enormous. It was terrible. He tried to force himself to think of other things, but every time his thoughts clicked back to the break-in his stomach clenched, he started to pant, his head jerked from side to side as if he could avoid the terror by looking away.

It was a blazing hot day again, but he felt clammy, stuck to his jeans and tee shirt. There was no Smithie lurking by the cemetery gates. He watched his feet moving, one-two, one-two. They seemed to have nothing to do with him. Whatever *he* thought about the matter, they were going to school. They'd take him with them, whether he wanted them to or not.

Albeson knew that he had to go, although he'd lain awake most of the night making wild and elaborate plans to run away. Every now and again, in his sleepy state, the desperate thoughts would turn into half-dreams. He'd be happy and relieved as he sailed into the blue waters of the South Seas on a white sailing ship. Then slowly the thought would prick into the softness of the dream: this can't be right; this can't be real. And suddenly, with a lurch of horror, he'd be fully awake, and groan and turn over in his hot, uncomfortable bed.

If he didn't go to school, after all that had happened over the last few days, he'd be finished. They'd know immediately. There'd be no doubt. Again and again in the night he'd drifted off and dreamed that he just simply didn't go to school. Each time the dream ended with two policemen, huge and bitter, hammering on the front door. Albeson wasn't in school. So Albeson had done it.

When he got to the gates he stood on the pavement opposite for a time. He found it hard to breathe. He felt odd, empty. Even at this point he might have turned and run away. But one of the doors opened and three teachers came out. They scanned the stragglers carefully, with grim, tense faces. Albeson pushed himself off from the kerb as though he was swimming away from a wreck with little hope of reaching the shore. He walked through the gates, across the yard, into the big stone entrance. The teachers stared at him. He stared at his feet. Tarmac, tarmac, tarmac, steps of concrete and stone. He was inside. No one had spoken.

There was an eerie, fantastic quietness inside the school. It was a hush that he could practically feel. Albeson almost jumped, it was so unusual. He lifted his eyes from his feet. Everyone was there all right, sitting in rows in the hall, most on the floor but some on chairs at the back. The babies were there too, silent as mice, with wide petrified eyes. Teachers stood around in the mass of children, like vultures in a littered desert, moving their heads from the neck, gazing about them, their bodies quite still. The silence was like electricity. It trembled in the air.

Albeson and the other stragglers sat down on the floor in the very front row. The others gazed round in awe, but his own eyes were fixed on the end wall, the huge, appalling stain spreading from high in the rafters down over the school motto and the blackboard. He did not dare even glance to left or right. He couldn't decide what looked more suspicious, to keep dead still or to stare about. He concentrated hard to try and stop panting. It was as if he'd run a mile. His chest was heaving. His blood was racing. He was very giddy.

When Mr Johnson walked onto the platform the spell of

69

silence wavered. There was a low sigh, a gasp of fearful wonder from the body of the hall. Mr Johnson was carrying a long, thin cane with a bent handle. A real cane, not the bamboo stick he kept on his wall. His face looked like stone. As he stared bleakly out at the sea of faces the sigh faded away. He stared and stared, the only movement in the hall his big bony hands flexing themselves round the prayer desk. The cane stuck out from one hand, pointing to the roof, quivering. The silence crept back.

'In this hall,' said Mr Johnson, 'there sits a boy or boys who will shortly be getting a taste of this.'

With a shockingly sudden movement he threw his right hand towards the back wall with enormous force. There was a whistle, a definite, high-pitched whistle, as the cane whipped through the air. From the hall there came another sigh, deeper and more hopeless than the first. It was like a groan. Albeson couldn't take his eyes off the cane, hanging now beside the headmaster's leg. It was so thin, so wickedly thin.

'And that, my fine young friends, is without doubt far and away the pleasantest thing that will happen to them.'

Mr Johnson bared his teeth in a sort of smile that made Albeson lick his lips. 'For when I have finished with that boy, or those boys,' he went on, in a slow, deep voice, 'he or they will be handed over to Her Majesty's police. In my long experience of such matters, I feel quite confident that those gentlemen will know what to do next. And after *that* there will be courts, magistrates, judges and juries – and the final awful clang as the prison gates close.'

He paused and leaned forward, his eyes boring into the children like hot pokers. He dropped his voice to a terrifying hiss.

'Those gates,' he said slowly, 'will not reopen for a very long time. A very . . . long . . . time . . . indeed.'

The children leaned forward as if they had been hypnotized. They stared into Mr Johnson's face. He stared back for long moments.

'For those of you who are not guilty,' he went on at last, 'I had better explain. Over the weekend this school was entered by a gang – I shall assume there were more than one of them from the amount of mindless destruction wrought – by a gang of half-witted oafs who went on a spree of vandalism. If any boy or girl moves so much as a muscle to look now I will beat them, but you will doubtless have noticed certain evidences of this hooliganism. In the classrooms, some of which will be unusable until extensive – and expensive – repair works have been carried out, the destruction was even more marked. And not only the fabric of our school has been damaged. The very heart of it, the soul of Church Street, has been violated and besmirched.'

Mr Johnson clenched his teeth with a snap and his eyes bulged. Albeson had no idea what the words meant, but he could not tear away his gaze. His mouth hung open. Mr Johnson went slowly red. The colour deepened until he was frighteningly purple. The muscles in his cheeks worked.

He let out his breath in a roar that shook the windows.

'It is DISGUSTING!'

This time there was not even a ripple of sound. A dead pause, silent except for the headmaster's breath, rasping and horrible. After a few seconds a girl in the babies started to whimper. A teacher shushed but it was no good. The whimper became a wail. As the little girl began to cry several others joined in, until there was a little bawling bunch in the middle of the hall. For Albeson and the older children it was terrible. The desire to cry, to join in, was overpowering. Albeson bit his lip and squeezed his eyes shut, fighting the tears with everything he'd got.

By the time the crying babies had been led out, Mr Johnson had gone back to normal. But he had not finished with them by a long chalk.

'As you all know,' he said, 'this is not the first time such goings-on have been recorded. I had cause to lecture you before, and that time I warned of the terrible consequences if it should ever happen again. Well, not only has it happened, but it has been done in such a way that the earlier incidents seem relatively minor. The country-dance room has been wrecked, the hall has been turned into a filthy den, and every classroom has in some way been damaged. Apart from anything else, my friends, the culprits will be faced with a bill running into hundreds, possibly thousands, of pounds.'

Some of the braver boys felt able to make noises of surprise now that the squalling babies had eased the tension. But Mr Johnson slammed the side of the desk with his cane. They shut up.

'There are some things that money cannot buy, however,' Mr Johnson went on. 'You children may have cats and dogs, some of you. Others may have white mice or guinea-pigs. Some of the teachers in this school let you pet, or stroke, or look at animals from time to time. I believe it is a good thing. We should all love living creatures, great or small. It is God's law.'

The strain was back. There was a new feeling of uncomfortableness now that God had been brought into it. Albeson's tongue moved on his lips once more.

'In Mrs Armstrong's class there was a tank of fish. Tropical fish of great worth and great beauty. She tells me that many of you spent many hours watching them. Mrs Armstrong loved her little fish very much.'

The headmaster paused. He seemed about to go red again, to shake with rage. Then he shrugged.

'I say "was" with meaning. For these filthy little oafs smashed that fish tank and killed the little fishes. Yes. Some boys sitting in front of me today left Mrs Armstrong's fish to flap and suffocate on the classroom floor. What do we think of that, eh?'

Whatever anyone else felt, Albeson felt awful. He knew his face was bright red. He wanted to die. But all round him other faces were red, other children shuffled guiltily on their haunches. It seemed that in some strange way everyone felt ashamed, everyone felt it had been them. Albeson had a vision of Smithie's blood-filled shoe leaking slowly into the pool of water. Little oafs, breaking God's law.

'Today, boys and girls,' said Mr Johnson, 'I am going to call in the police. I expect you will all know the term C.I.D. from your television viewing. It is short for Criminal Investigation Department. Today the Criminal Investigation Department of the city police will be sending along some detectives. As you can imagine, the culprits will be found in very short order. Then this disgusting business will be made an end of for good and all.'

He paused for quite a time to let the news sink in. People were beginning to look seriously frightened now. There were whimpers coming from several of the older girls and a lot of white faces among the top boys. Mr Johnson rapped his knuckles on the desk in a brisk, business-like way.

'There is one way we can avoid all this nastiness,' he said. 'The culprits can give themselves up. The results for them will be just the same in the end; they must be punished. But the police, and the magistrates, and the education authorities, are bound to take into account a truthful and courageous act, however late it is in coming. I can say with all truthfulness that it would be better for everybody if the boys concerned will own up.'

There was a general shuffling. Some people looked around them, others stared at the floor. At least half the children looked as though they had done it. Even some of the teachers seemed very ill at ease. After a minute the headmaster spoke again.

'I will make one more plea for honesty,' he said. 'And I will also make an offer. If the culprits will stand up here and now I will not cane them. They must face the consequences of their acts of course. But the first part of their punishment I will drop.' He waved the cane so that it swished gently. 'You have two minutes,' he said.

As the seconds crept by Albeson almost burst with the effort not to confess. He dug his fingernails deeper and deeper into his palms, his eyes were screwed up so tight it hurt badly. It would have been so lovely to just stand up and say the words. He knew that a great weight would have fallen from him, that he would have felt light, and clean, and loved. Every part of him ached to admit it, his lungs ached to rid themselves of the breathless pain he was suffering.

When Mr Johnson said 'Fifteen seconds' Albeson actually tried to stand up and speak. But the part of his mind that was fighting the confession turned the movement into a painful jerk and the sound into a strangled gurgle. A little girl burst into tears nearby and no one noticed Albeson's tortured face.

'Right,' said Mr Johnson, grimly. 'That is that then. If the culprits wish, they can come to my room in private. By lunch time it will be too late. Carry on please, teachers.'

He turned on his heel and strode off the platform, his shoulders square, the cane slapping his legs. As he left a real row broke out for a short while. Girls bawled, boys let out their breath in whistling gasps or giggled as though they'd die, teachers shouted. Albeson remained on the floor, exhausted and limp, brushing away at his eyes as the few tears squeezed themselves out.

It wasn't until much later, in the temporary classroom where Mrs Armstrong's class had been put, that Albeson realized that Pam's spell had worked. There were no Germans. It was a weird sensation, of worry and relief. The headmaster's speech had been terrible and he was scared to the bottom of his shoes of being found out still, but the spell had worked. The Germans had not come. All the doubts that Smithie had raised in his mind about her went away. Pammy *was* a witch. She would save him whatever happened. He thought about the detectives coming. *If* she had time!

There wasn't much teaching done all day. Mrs Armstrong did her best to quieten down the class but she was obviously tense and jumpy herself. Two of the girls kept crying on and off over the fate of the fish, while some of the boys were morbidly fascinated to know all the details of their deaths. She didn't want to talk about it, but the kids kept coming back to the subject and worrying it. In the end she started shouting every time anyone moved. Gary Carstairs, who never knew when to stop, got smacked round the head, which was most unlike Mrs Armstrong.

By the end of the afternoon Albeson had still not seen the detectives, although rumour had it that they were definitely in Church Street and they were following a series of easy clues. When the bell went at three-thirty everyone, including Albeson, was vaguely surprised and vaguely disappointed. There had been no arrest. When they'd got over the let-down feeling the fierce discussion broke out. Everybody asked 'Miss' if someone would be arrested in the morning.

But 'Miss' was busy cornering Albeson before he could sneak off. She wanted to talk to him.

His feeling of doom deepened as the last kids trailed out. He fidgeted madly, trying to be calm. The pain in his chest was coming back. She knew. She obviously knew. This was the end then. This was what it felt like.

Mrs Armstrong closed the classroom door with a bang. She stopped in front of him and looked into his face. Albeson, miserable and guilty, dropped his eyes.

'Is there anything you want to say, Jimmy?' she said quietly.

'No, Miss,' he muttered.

A pause.

'Oh. I had the feeling that you wanted to say something to me. Was I wrong?'

He could feel the tears prickling the backs of his eyes, but the pressure to blurt out the truth was nothing like it had been under Mr Johnson's reign of terror. He just couldn't think of a way off the hook, that was all.

Mrs Armstrong spoke again. 'A lot of people think you could have been involved in what happened, Jimmy. What do you say to that?'

Nothing. Absolutely nothing. He waited for the blow to fall.

'But I don't. I don't think you're that kind of a boy. Not the kind of boy who would kill those poor . . .'

He interrupted her. He'd had a brainwave.

'Please, Miss, where are the Germans? That's what I wanted to ask. Where are they? Why didn't they come to school?'

She stared at him, surprised. Then she gave a little laugh.

'Oh the Germans. Hans and Erica. Well the headmaster phoned Mr Grundmann I suppose. I mean they couldn't start on a day like today, could they? My classroom – *our* classroom – is a . . . Well, those boys made quite a mess I can tell you.'

Albeson tried to restrain his excitement.

'Will they be able to come at all? Will they go to another school? Will he take 'em away?'

'Take them away? Good Lord no! Oh no, Jimmy, nothing like that. They'll just have to start a few days late that's all. It's the middle of term so it doesn't really matter, does it?'

Albeson didn't answer.

'And there's another thing too, of course. I'd forgotten it in all the fuss over the break-in. Mr Grundmann would very much like you to go to tea with them on Wednesday. Is that all right? And, Jimmy – let's have no more nonsense about them shall we? None of this silly war nonsense?'

Albeson wriggled in every way he knew how. He said it wasn't possible but he couldn't say why. He said his mum was ill but Mrs Armstrong knew it was untrue. He said his dad wouldn't let him but he couldn't give a reason.

Mrs Armstrong said coolly: 'I'll come and ask him myself, Jimmy. I'll come along tonight.'

Albeson was aghast. She was mad. She'd had one brush with his father, seen what he could be like. She couldn't go round there again. He'd half kill her! He tried to speak but only stuttered.

'What did you say, Jimmy? You'll have to speak up. If you can't tell me Wednesday will be all right I'll talk to your father. I'll come home with you now.'

'No!' said Albeson. 'Wednesday. Yes. I'll come. Yes.' He couldn't stand the shame if his father was rude again. He couldn't stand the shame.

'Are you sure it's all right? You'll have to ask your parents and tell me tomorrow.'

'Yes.'

He blurted out: 'Have they got a dog? The Germans?'

'A dog? Well yes, I think they have. Yes, they have, called Fritz. Why, you funny boy?'

Mrs Armstrong gave him a puzzled smile. His lips quivered. If only she knew how much he hated her!

Chapter 10

Coming out of school was like coming up from drowning. Albeson stood on the pavement and shook himself. The air smelt clean and the roaring traffic seemed friendly. He looked all round him, not quite knowing what to do or where to go. The lollipop lady called to him 'Come on, dear, I haven't got all night to wait for stragglers.' Ah well, he wasn't particular which way he went. He waited till she'd stopped the urgent tea-time traffic and wandered across the road. As he passed the phone box Pammy hissed at him.

'Albeson! Over here! Where you *been*? I've been waiting for *ages*!'

His heart sank. Pammy's freckly face was anxious. She pushed her hair back with a dirty hand.

'They're after Smithie,' she whispered. 'The police. They've been round his uncle's and they're searching the town. Come on, quick.'

She reached for his arm but Albeson drew back. Come on where, come on what?

'Don't hang about, Albeson. You're in this too you know. If they catch Smithie you're as good as done.'

He stared at her dumbly. She smiled at him. Although she looked urgent, anxious, he could see that in some strange way she was enjoying herself. Her eyes were very bright. She hopped from one foot to the other.

'He wouldn't tell on me,' he said, not believing it. His voice trembled. 'He's my mate. Smithie's my mate.'

'Mate or no mate he'd have to tell, stands to reason. Crikey, Albeson, they're the *police*! They don't mess about do they? 'Course he'd tell. They'd make him.'

Albeson looked over his shoulder. Mr Kowalski, the caretaker, was clearing up the schoolyard. In all the traffic, in the broad sunshine, facing Pam in her long dirty dress and white plastic boots, he felt very lonely.

'Where is he then?' he asked.

Pam leaned towards him. She cupped her hand behind his ear and whispered.

'I can't tell you,' she said dramatically. 'Just follow me.

'And Albeson,' she added a second later, putting her hand back beside his head, 'keep your eyes peeled for coppers. They're everywhere.'

She went by the queerest route possible, but Albeson soon guessed where they were heading for. She made him look casually in the Albert Road shops, they wandered in and out of Woolies twice, she told him to go into the men's lavatory in George Street although he didn't need to. But in the end it was obvious. There weren't that many ways you could approach Fatty Hill's.

Getting in was easy. Pammy had made an exit hole in the rotten corrugated iron opposite a derelict pub. It was covered with scrubby bushes. They looked up and down the abandoned street for a few seconds, then squeezed through the narrow, jagged gap.

'It's a good hole that,' she said proudly. 'They'll never find that with a bit of luck. Took me ages it did.'

When they got to the Cadillac Albeson couldn't see Smithie. Pammy played her masterstroke. She tip-toed up to the wreck and tapped on the bonnet. She tapped several times, in a code.

'That's so he knows it's us,' she told Albeson. 'He's holding it closed from inside.'

When she opened the bonnet, however, the engine space

79

was empty. Smithie crawled out from under an old Austin, ten feet away.

Pam was furious.

'You fool,' she said. 'You could've spoilt everything. What d'you do that for?'

Smithie was bright red and sweating. His voice was very quiet, sort of fed up and tired.

'Too hot,' he muttered. 'I thought I was going to pass out. It must be a hundred degrees in there.'

Albeson stared at his friend as he sat down on the car's wing. He was in a terrible state. The sore on his lip had been picked till it was raw. He was covered in dust and grease from hiding in the dump. He was soaking wet. His trouser legs, from the knees down, were all wrinkled and peculiar, the right one with a long tear in it. Albeson was amazed he could still walk, let alone anything else. He couldn't make out any dried blood on the shoe, but it seemed a bit darker than the left one.

'Hallo, Smithie,' he said, not sure of himself at all. 'What's up then?'

Smithie just looked at the ground.

'Everything's up,' he said, hardly opening his mouth. 'We've done it this time, nipper. We're in for it.'

Albeson couldn't think of a reply. Somehow it struck him as being rotten unfair. *He'd* done hardly anything. It was Smithie's fault. Smithie had gone barmy that was all. He'd never have done it on his own. He'd never have killed the fish.

'What we going to do?' he asked at last.

Smithie shook his head, muttering. He started on his lip again, pulling at it savagely. It was nasty to watch but you couldn't help watching. Albeson was lonely again. He could hear the world outside Fatty Hill's and he wanted to go and join it. But he couldn't. They'd done it this time. When he spoke his voice came out all hissy and weak, not at all how he'd meant it to.

'What'll happen now, Pammy? What'll they do if they catch us?'

Pammy was on the ground, drawing patterns with a stair rod. A thin, brass-covered one, of the sort that killed Daniel Bullock.

'Dunno,' she said. 'I bet you'll go to prison though. Smithie will anyway. You might be too young.'

'How old d'you have to be? What'll they do if I'm too young to go?' His voice was eager.

Pam soon dashed his hopes.

'You won't get off with it, Jimmy,' she said. 'If they send Smithie away they won't just let you off. There'll be somewhere, borstal or detention or something. I don't know.'

He didn't want to go. There was a snuffling sound. Smithie was crying, licking the tears with a big pink tongue as they ran past his nose.

'I don't want to go away again,' he said jerkily, between crying and licking. 'I don't want to. I'm fed up with it. I ain't going to be sent away again.'

They let this sink in without saying anything. Albeson wondered why he'd been sent away before, but not enough to ask. Being sent away seemed remote, distant, unreal. But believable. He didn't want to go.

Pammy got up abruptly and climbed into the Cadillac's engine compartment. He listened idly to the clanks and grunts from within. After a minute or two she popped out, greasy and sweaty. Albeson was sweating too. It was very hot; muggy and sticky.

'Crikey it's hot in there,' said Pam brightly. 'You were right, Smithie.'

She jumped over the side to the ground and did a surprising thing. She reached into her cardigan pocket – Pammy always wore a cardigan, rain or heatwave – and pulled out two bars of chocolate. They were soft, melted into their wrappers. She gave one to Albeson and tapped Smithie's hand with the other. He stopped pulling at his lip. He looked puzzled. He stopped crying.

'Come on, Smithie, cheer up,' said Pammy. Her voice was jolly, she was grinning cheerfully. 'It's not the end of the world. Have a chockie bar and shut your row, you big cissie. I expect you're just hungry, that's all.'

She accepted one sticky square from each of them but nothing more. When they'd finished licking the runny off their lips and fingers she laughed. Albeson felt a lot better. Smithie too, by the look of him.

'Just what the doctor ordered eh? Trust your Auntie Pam. I nicked 'em in Woolies right under your nose, Jimmy. You are a slow one! Now listen. Smithie, sit down against that wheel. Albeson, you lean over there. I've got a plan.'

When she'd arranged them as she wanted Pam took one last glance round the dump to make sure Old Nobbler wasn't creeping up on them. She crouched in front of the boys, her skirt arranged over her knees. She talked fast and low.

'I've looked at my crystal ball even though I didn't really need to,' she said. 'You'd have to be a fool not to see what's to be done. But it did help in one way. If you do like I say you'll be all right. You won't get caught and you won't get sent away. All right?'

Albeson nodded, his eyes on Pam's lively freckled face.

'Right, well for starters you've got to run away. It's as plain as the nose on your face. The police are after Smithie and he can't live the rest of his life in Fatty Hill's. As for Albeson, well the same thing goes. After what you two did in the school they'll never rest till they catch you. If you make it too hard for them they'll bring in the dogs. You wouldn't like that now, would you, kid?'

Albeson shivered.

'You was right about the Germans, Pammy,' he said. 'They have got a dog. Miss said.'

''Course I was right,' said Pammy. 'An alsatian. Just like the police tracker dogs. Attack first and ask questions afterwards. I'm right about everything, you'll see.'

Smithie said miserably: 'We can't run away. Where'll we go to? We've not got no fares. We've not got no food. They'll catch us.'

'That's just what I'm saying,' said Pam irritably. 'I've consulted the crystal. If you stay here you'll get caught all right. If you run away you'll be okay.'

'Crystal ball!' Smithie spat the words out. 'That's just an old bearing or something. Who d'you think you're kidding?'

Albeson was shocked. He watched Pammy's face. She smiled easily.

'Get out of it, Smithie,' she said. 'You ask Albeson. Were the Germans there today, kid? *Were* they?'

He shook his head.

'There you are then. And what stopped them eh? Do *you* know Smithie? I'll tell you. It was me. Me and that crystal ball.

'Anyway,' she went on before Albeson could explain any more, 'what else can you do? You know you've done it now, Brian Smith. You've got to run away. So's Albeson. You've got yourselves in lumber. You'll get sent away, the both of you.'

'There's detectives in the school, Smithie,' Albeson said quietly. 'Everyone reckons there'll be an early arrest. And ... and . . .' (this had only just occurred to him; he felt horror creeping through him as he realized it) 'there's lots reckon I was in on it. Miss told me. The teachers think it was me.'

'Yes,' said Pammy kindly. 'Well it's not surprising is it, Albeson? It *was* you, you dope!'

He almost yelled: It was Smithie! It was Smithie! He killed the fish! I didn't do anything! But he kept his mouth shut. Oh it was awful.

After a long pause Smithie muttered: 'Where we going to run to though? That's the question.'

'Easy,' said Pam. 'You'll have to go to London. Once you get to London you'll be all right. It's big, millions and millions of people. No one'll ever find you there.'

'Go on,' said Smithie dully. 'How we going to get there?'

'You hitch,' said Pam. She'd got it all worked out.

Albeson hoped she was right. But then she always was. He felt a stir of excitement. London. It was better than borstal, anyway.

'Listen,' she said, waggling Smithie's knee with her hand. 'What do you want, Smithie? To stay here and get done or go to London and start clean? What's anyone ever give you here eh? What's the big attraction about this dump? Go to London and you'll be a new bloke. Stay here and you know just what'll happen.'

He picked at his lip.

'Oh come on, Smithie, you ghost. It'll be fun. London's fantastic. You'll get a job like a shot. Earn money. Work in a fair or something. It's easy in London. Everyone goes there when they're in lumber. It's the place. Everything's easy in London.'

Albeson was definitely feeling quite excited now. He looked at Smithie, willing him to join in the idea. Crikey Moses, anything was better than going to prison.

'All right,' said Pam at last. 'If you want to go to jail that's your lookout. But think about Albeson. He's your friend. He's only a kid. I bet you did most of the mess in the school, Smithie, that's what I bet. And poor little Albeson's going to get done for it is he? What sort of a mate are you when it comes to it, eh?'

Albeson was frightened by this. He wouldn't have dared say it in case Smithie took it wrong. He waited for the flare-up, for Pammy to get smashed. After a couple of seconds he glanced at Smithie. His friend smiled at him, and there were tears in his eyes.

'I'm sorry, mate, honest I am,' he muttered. 'I didn't mean to get you in it, Albeson. I'll see you right, nipper, honest I will. We'll go to London and I'll look after you. We'll be all right, you see.'

Pammy laughed happily. She was beaming from ear to ear. Albeson shivered. He felt desperately lonely. He wanted his mum and dad, something rotten he wanted them. But that was that.

Chapter 11

It was a strange feeling, completely new to him, but it didn't stop. Over the next couple of hours he kept swooping from the heights of excitement to the depths of despair. He had no control over it, but it did seem to Albeson that when he was up Smithie was down. When his friend started to get cheerful again, he tended to get gloomy. The weather didn't help. It was definitely thundery now. He had a vague headache. It was much too hot. The air didn't move about like it ought to have done; more like treacle.

While Pam was away getting them food and any money she could scrounge from her family, they talked about London. Once the idea had taken hold in Smithie's mind he seemed to have worked it out pretty quickly. He knew a lot about London, it turned out. His Uncle Frank went there often, something to do with the flower shop although he didn't quite know what. Getting a job was a piece of cake, apparently – like falling off a log. It was the capital of the country (even Albeson knew that much) where most of the foreigners lived, and every other person was only passing through. Because of this, said Smithie, you didn't need papers or 'cards' or anything. You just went along to someone who was looking for help and got signed up on the spot. Pay was good too, it being the capital. That was on account of everything being very dear there, fur coats and jewellery and so on.

'I don't see how we can get a job,' Albeson put in. 'We're

not old enough. I mean you might get by all right, but what about me?'

Smithie thought about this a bit.

'Tell you what,' he said finally, 'I bet I can pass for eighteen. I'll get a job down the docks and earn enough to keep us both. They earn a fortune in London, the dockies do. They're all communists.'

This sounded fair enough, although Albeson hadn't even known London had a docks. He thought it was an inland place.

'I wish you could get to be a lorry driver,' he said. 'Then I could be your mate. Hey, Smithie, that'd be smashing.'

'Well I might at that,' Smithie replied. 'I mean they reckon you can do anything in London. You don't need papers at all. I might have a try at any rate.'

'You can't drive a lorry can you?' asked Albeson. 'Get off with you, you can't!'

'Well I 'aven't got a licence if that's what you mean, but it can't be that hard can it? I mean, we've watched them at it enough, down at the Camber and Flathouse.'

Fair enough again. Albeson often imagined himself at the wheel of a big lorry. He knew all the gear positions, and which pedals were the clutch, brake and accelerator. He was going to be a lorry driver one day, he was sure of that. And he didn't think it would take much learning, what with all his years of watching. Smithie too, very likely.

'Yeah, if I could get behind the wheel of one I'd be all right. And we could reckon you was a midget. We could say you was forty-three! Then they'd have to let you be my mate!'

They fell about at this, and played midget lorry drivers among the wrecked cars for a while. Albeson was still happy as a lark when Smithie said gloomily: 'She's not coming back you know, nipper. She must've been nabbed by her old lady.'

Albeson thought about it while Smithie brooded. It was

quite likely. Pammy was always getting nabbed by someone in her family. She said that was why her ears were so big – because they kept getting pulled. At any rate she'd been gone a rotten long time. The noise of the traffic was lower. He looked up at the sun, hazed in cloud now, although it was hotter than it had been if anything. It was getting late. It must be well after tea-time. He might have been missed at home, he thought.

'What we going to do then, Smithie?' he asked. 'We can't hang around too long. If we're going we'd better go eh?'

'She's a bloody sod,' said Smithie savagely. 'She got us in this mess, nipper. Now she can't even be bothered to get us some grub.'

Albeson didn't argue. Smithie was in a rage, flouncing around the dump kicking at things. On the force of the rage they swept out of Fatty Hill's through the newly-made hole and set out for the big roundabout. It was quite a long walk but Smithie never spoke once. He kept up a cracking pace, despite the fact that his cut leg made him limp. He was glowering angrily and his lips moved all the time as though he was swearing under his breath.

The roundabout was monstrous. It led out of the town, out of the island, to all places north, east and west. Cars raced round it at speed, their tyres squealing as they leaned over. The pavement shook as heavy lorries thundered to and from the docks. Buses rumbled past more slowly, and there seemed to be an amazing number of coaches carrying holidaymakers in to the resort or out on mainland pleasure jaunts. There were four lanes, all of them absolutely jammed with traffic. The noise, the fumes, the heat were terrific. Albeson's head swam.

He leaned against the parapet of the bridge smelling the clean, seaweedy smell of the creek which wafted over it. There was a definite line, you could feel it, where the fumes and heat stopped and the sea smell began. A line of air, roughly on top of the parapet. Every now and again it wavered as a breath of wind moved in the sickly air.

Smithie did the thumbing, standing right on the edge of the streams of traffic. Albeson alternately looked over the bridge, watched the lorries go by, and kept an eye open for cop cars. Whenever he saw the lurid red and white, topped off with a blue light, he shouted to Smithie. Then they'd look out dreamily over the parapet, their faces well hidden, their hearts drumming, until the car flashed past the corners of their eyes and out of sight.

Nobody stopped.

After about an hour Smithie wandered over to Albeson and they sat down on the hot pavement, backs to the concrete slats that let in the cooler, sea-smelly air. Smithie sighed.

'It's just not our day, nipper, it's just not our day. Not one of them's even slowed down. At this rate it'll be next Thursday week before we get to London.'

He didn't appear to be particularly worried by it. Albeson looked at him, curious to know what sort of mood he was in. He, Albeson, felt strangely peaceful. There was something soothing about the constant roaring of the traffic. The constant waves of hot, fumy air pushed into his face by the swathes of vehicles made him feel slightly sleepy, vaguely content.

'Tell you what,' said Smithie. 'Let's go to the pictures!'

That was a surprise.

'What you talking about?' he said. 'We're on the run! The cops are after us.'

'All the more reason,' said Smithie. 'They'll never think of looking for us in there. People on the run don't stop off and go to the pictures, now do they?'

Maybe not, but it was still a daft idea. So what though? He fancied going to the pictures, it wasn't often he got the chance.

Smithie went on: 'Anyway, nipper, I'm not stupid. I don't mean *just* go to the flicks. After we've come out there'll be less traffic. More chance of getting picked up when you think about it. I mean it stands to reason no one would stop here. It's too crowded for a kick-off.'

It flashed through Albeson's mind that Smithie could have thought of that a bit earlier. Standing on a roundabout had struck him as being odd anyway. How was anyone to know which of all the roads off it you wanted to go up? He said nothing.

Smithie must have thought he still wasn't convinced.

'Even if we don't get picked up here, after, we could go down the docks. If we went down the Camber we could ask a lorry driver, an overnight one. We'd be *bound* to get a lift then. Straight to London. Straight to London docks even! Then I could get a job straight away! On the spot! Hey, fantastic!'

It turned out, when they got to the Odeon, that Smithie had only enough money to get himself in, so they had to work the emergency exit trick. First of all they walked round the back, to the big quiet car park, to choose a door. Two of them were a bit too easily seen from the houses behind the cinema, but one was ideal. It was in a recess at the corner of the big oblong building. The actual door, painted red and without markings, was set about four feet into the recess, so that nobody would see you unless they looked straight into it. There were quite a few cars parked, but no people around at all.

'Righto then,' said Smithie. 'I'll go in and get a seat up-stairs. You hang on down here until you hear three taps. Then you tap three times so I know there's no one about and I'll open up the push-bar for you. All right? If you don't tap I'll hang on a bit then tap again. Don't tap till it's all clear. Got it?'

"Course I've got it, you big ghost,' said Albeson. 'Go on hurry up, or we'll miss the rotten picture won't we.'

When Smithie had crunched off round the corner of the building Albeson set himself up to wait. He scanned the car park carefully to make sure he wasn't too obvious. It was lined with thick rough hedges, quite high, the odd tree sticking out of the middle. Behind the hedges there were houses, posh-looking semis of the sort his mum mentioned from time to time as like the one they were soon going to be living in. He squinted through his fingers to get a better view of the windows. But they were reflecting the late sun, dulled by clouds now but still strong enough to practically blind him. Oh well, if anyone was watching they probably wouldn't know what was going on. Even if they did they'd probably not bother to report him. Suddenly Albeson started to pant as he remembered the awful trouble he was in. To be arrested for getting into the pictures free would just about put the tin lid on it. Smashing up the school, playing in Fatty Hill's, stealing chockie bars from Woolworths, running away . . .

A car full of people drew up in front of him and took his mind off it luckily. It was a big Vauxhall, mother, father and three kids. The kids were making quite a row, larking about, the little girl – she was about six – making a real nuisance of herself. Her father made a grab at her and Albeson flinched. But instead of hitting her he swung her through the air and somehow landed her on his shoulders, her legs sticking out from each side of his head. They went round the front laughing.

After that Albeson counted up to three hundred. The sun got dimmer and more cars arrived. He wanted to go to the lavatory and he rather fancied something to eat as well. It was getting a bit of a strain. Every time a car arrived he had to look casual, find something to do, as if he was just a kid looking at a wall or something. He was getting panicky.

It was ages before he admitted to himself that Smithie had done the dirty on him. The car park was almost full and the windows opposite had lost the sun completely. That was one thing, there was certainly no one keeping an eye on him. But what did that matter? There was no law against standing in a cinema car park, or even an emergency exit. Smithie had gone in and forgotten him.

Albeson didn't know what to do. He was intensely miserable. First Pam and now Smithie. He thought of the things Smithie had said about Pammy. Was it true? Could it be true? Pammy liked Albeson, she was always coming to find him. She'd done the spell to stop the Germans coming. She'd found out about the car crash on the bombed-site. But she never came into the school herself and she'd not turned up with their sandwiches. Smithie said she liked to drop people in it. No, not Pammy. He liked Pammy.

Then he thought about Smithie. He wasn't meant to play with him. Why not? Smithie was all right. But Derek laughed at him, called him a big kid. What was wrong with that? Kids were all right too, weren't they? But in the school Smithie had frightened him. He remembered the stains on Smithie's shirt. Black with sweat, smelling awful, strong, catching his throat. That was the trouble with Smithie; you never knew where you were with him. Blood dribbling over the top of his shoe, the pinky red stain in the water, the flapping fish, bright and gasping.

He didn't know where he was going to go, but all at once Albeson knew he was off. As his foot left the ground, as he turned to leave the recess, there were three taps at the door.

Chapter 12

Albeson stood quite still, with one foot actually raised from the ground. It was in his mind to run, to just go, to zoom off. But in the end he turned back to the door and tapped three times. There was a clank and a bang as the emergency push-bar was pushed. Smithie appeared, red in the face but smiling.

' Sorry about that, nipper. Get in quick, it's started. Smashing it is, too, a cowboy. There was a Bugs Bunny too. Aergh, what's up, Doc?'

On the way up the long staircase Smithie explained what had happened. When he'd bought his ticket and gone upstairs there had only been three other people in. He'd sat dead close to the exit but the usherette had been watching him like a hawk. Once he'd gone out through the curtains but she'd followed. He'd had to pretend he was looking for the gents. Then when she pointed it out to him he'd had to go there and hang about for a while.

'Crikey,' said Albeson. 'What happened? Did she go away?'

'Nah,' said Smithie. 'I was dead worried, Albie. I thought you'd be thinking I'd done the dirty on you, like that Pammy.'

Albeson blushed.

'Don't talk daft,' he said hotly. 'It was all right out there, watching the cars. I knew you'd come in the end. Hey, there was an MG come after you'd gone. Smashing.'

'Anyway,' Smithie went on, 'I kept looking at her and she kept her eyes on me, and I thought we'd really had it. But after the adverts and that the place started to fill up. I changed seats a couple of times too, so as to mix her up like, then the ice-cream girl come round. In the end she didn't know if she was coming or going. After Bugs I watched the start of the cowboy then nipped out. She was still taking tickets. We'll have to get back in sharpish though.'

'What was the Bugs Bunny like?' said Albeson. He liked Bugs Bunny better than anything.

'Smashing,' said Smithie. 'It had Daffy Duck in and that little bald bloke. There was this pond and they kept on blowing each other up.'

'Seen it,' said Albeson. He was pleased. Hate to have missed one he didn't know.

'Sssh!' said Smithie. They'd reached the top of the stairs.

Before they pushed open the swing door they did two things. First of all Smithie gave Albeson his ticket.

'She's already asked me for it,' he explained. 'So if she asks again she can whistle. I'll tell her I've lost it. She won't have a leg to stand on.'

Then they waited. This was Smithie's second idea.

'It's a cowboy see. When they start shooting, or the Indians yell or something, everyone'll be watching the screen, her an' all. Then we'll sneak in. Got it?'

They could tell when it was going to happen because of the way the music got all loud and exciting. As it turned out it was shooting, sounding odd and hollow through the swing doors and curtain.

'Come on,' said Smithie, and they crept in. Not a head turned as they crabbed their way along the back, all eyes were glued to the action. Smithie slipped into his seat after making sure the usherette was not watching. Albeson took a seat near him, right on the back row. Nobody even seemed to notice. There were enough people in to make an extra little boy practically invisible. He tensed up as the girl looked round at last, but after a glance she turned her eyes to the front again. He was safe. He stretched his legs and relaxed, drinking in the warm dusty smell that he liked so much.

Apart from Saturday morning pictures that he sometimes went to if he had the money, Albeson hardly ever got to see the flicks. But he loved them all the more for that. It was the heat, and the smell, and the comfort of the folding seats, as well as the big colourful screen – so much better than the telly, which you watched anyway with mum talking and dad blowing fag smoke in your face, sat on the floor more than likely. It was especially nice to go with Smithie, because it was a racing cert he'd buy you an ice-cream in the interval. Albeson wondered if he had enough money left. Perhaps they'd have just one, and share it.

It was a good film too – the Odeon had an 'oldies' night every Monday, which was probably why so many people decided to go, including Smithie! – followed by an even better one. The cowboy was a bit slushy in parts, with a blonde-haired son trying for ages to rescue his father from some Indians. Albeson wouldn't have bothered, partly because he'd have rather been an Indian anyway; they seemed to him to be a lot better on their horses and he fancied living in a tent. Also there was a soppy woman in it with a long skirt who kept crying and kissing people. But the second picture was 'Treasure Island', which he'd never seen, and the man who played Long John Silver rolled his eyes and had a parrot and was just about the most fantastic person Albeson could ever remember. They did have an ice-cream as well, which they did share, dip and dip about with the little plastic shovel.

He was full of the colour and excitement of John Silver and 'Jim lad' at the end. He stood for the National Anthem in a daze, his mind still sailing the blue waters in search of more treasure. It must have been terrific to have been a boy in those days. Jim Hawkins crouched in the apple barrel as the pirate's knife hovered above his head. Fabulous!

They were still jabbering about it as they dropped down the big marble stairs and went boldly through the plushy entrance hall to the street.

It was raining. It wasn't just raining, it was chucking it down.

'Crikey, nipper. Here's a turn-up for the books!'

They stood in the foyer watching the solid water sheeting down through the orange street lights. There was no question of going outside. They didn't even have coats on, except Smithie's sports jacket. Every now and again some little group would push open one of the swing doors and dart out into a car or a taxi that had drawn up. Then the doorman started making it pretty obvious that he wanted to shut up for the night. Everyone slowly went outside and stood on the steps. After a while Smithie and Albeson were alone. The lights inside the cinema entrance went out. There was a roll of thunder, not loud, quite a long way off.

'What we going to do?' Albeson said at last. 'It's pouring down. We'll never get to the Camber in this, we'd be drownded.'

He was cold and his legs had got damp with the rain splashing up onto the steps. He was hungry too, rotten starving. He wanted to go home.

'It's a pig ain't it? You're dead right. We'll have to wait till it stops before we go there.'

'Have you got any bus money?'

'Nah. Spent it all on that ice-cream. Got two p that's all.'

The rain beat down. It was amazing that it could go on so hard so long.

'Smithie . . . ?' Albeson didn't really know what he was going to say, but he didn't dare go on, anyway.

'What?'

'Nothing.' A pause. 'I just thought . . .'

'What?'

'Nothing.'

Smithie grabbed his arm. He dug his fingers in until it hurt.

'Listen, Albeson,' he said. 'We ain't going whining back home if that's what you was thinking. You rotten little mummy's boy. You're yellow!'

Albeson could only give a low cry. Smithie was hurting like mad.

'You just think about it, you little cry-baby. The cops are after us. You as well, remember. You did it just as much as me. You chucked enough ink round Church Street to get sent away for years. And they've already been round my house. They know who they're after, got it?' He shook Albeson. 'Got it?'

'You're hurting! Smithie, let go my arm, you're hurting!'

Smithie let go and Albeson nursed his arm, whimpering. Smithie went on in a much quieter way.

'Anyway, nipper, look at it this way. What would your old man do if you waltzed in now eh? He'd give you such a belting you'd never get over it. Wouldn't he, eh?'

It was true. But maybe it would be better than this lot. He shivered. Maybe not.

'Another thing, you ghost. Where d'you think I got that money for the pictures? I nicked it from my Uncle Frank. And he told me last week that if I nicked any more there'd be trouble.'

Nicked it. That had never occurred to Albeson.

'We all know what trouble means don't we, nipper? He's only waiting for an excuse that's all. I'm a big drag to Uncle Frank. He'd send me away again soon as look at me. He knows how much I've been nicking. He knows.'

The traffic was thinning out a bit. A bus went past full. It must be getting dead late, thought Albeson. What a mess. He watched the rain. It was no longer bouncing off the pavement like exploding bombs. It was easing off.

A few minutes later Smithie took his wrist, not roughly this time, and led him into the drizzle. He set out very briskly, Albeson trotting to keep up. He was panting by the time they reached the derelict streets next to Fatty Hill's.

It was very eerie there at night. The boarded up houses looked dangerous in the dim light reflecting off the glistening blackness of the roads. A lot of the lamps had broken bulbs anyway – Albeson had thrown some of the stones himself. The high, jagged fence surrounding the dump was black and evil, the strands of barbed wire dripping as they swayed in the gentle wind.

'What are we going to do?' he asked Smithie.

'Stay here the night. In the Cadillac. It's dry in there and them seats are just like beds. We'll get up dead early, nip down the Camber, and hitch an early lorry up to London. Piece of cake.'

'What, go in? In Fatty Hill's? Not likely!'

He was terrified. Fatty Hill's was haunted, it was a well-known fact. All sorts of dreadful things had gone on in there one way and another. And the last person Albeson wanted to meet was Daniel Bullock, wandering about with a stair-rod through his heart.

'Why not, you daft haporth? Stands to reason don't it? No one'll come looking for us in there in the dead of night. They wouldn't dream of it. And we can't stand here in the rotten rain much longer. We'll catch our death of cold.'

Albeson dug in his heels. They stood outside the abandoned pub in the drizzle, arguing in frantic hisses. Finally he admitted that he was afraid of the ghosts. Smithie laughed really loud, frightening Albeson even worse.

'Shut up, you fool, shut up! You'll have someone after us!'

'Ghosts!' spluttered Smithie. 'You'd believe anything you would, nipper. That Pammy! She could twist you round her little finger!'

He felt uncomfortable. Every time Pam was mentioned now she showed up in a bad light. She'd always seemed so smashing too. Smithie suddenly put his arm round him and hugged him.

'Listen, Albie,' he said. 'God's honour there's no ghosts in Fatty Hill's. There's no such thing, I swear on my mother's grave. Pammy's a rotten little liar and she was having you on. All right?'

Albeson was confused. He buried his face in Smithie's jacket. It stank of wet wool. He didn't know what to do. He just wanted to lie down, to go to sleep.

'All right,' he said. 'We'll go in.'

'Good old nipper!' said Smithie. 'That's my little mate. You ain't scared of anything, are you kid?'

They looked up and down the road just to make sure, then went across to the bush that hid the new hole. The leaves were soaking, holding huge drops of glistening water. Smithie shook them to one side and squeezed through, grumbling to himself.

'It's rotten dark in here,' he said. 'I wish we had a torch. I've cut my hand. Go careful, I'll guide you through.'

As Albeson thrust himself into the bush a movement away to his right made him stiffen. He stared along the sagging fence. There was something coming round the corner of the dump!

'Smithie!' he hissed.

Then the barking started. The brown and white dog flashed under the street light halfway along the fence, going like a rocket. As Albeson jerked backwards a bent form appeared in the pool of light. His head was down, his bow legs were working like pistons, his lumpy stick was pointing ahead like a cutlass.

'Smithie! Get out quick! Get out! It's Old Nobbler!'

The dog was close. Albeson's stomach churned with terror. He turned and ran, his feet slipping in the mud, great splashes of water flying round him as he raced through deep puddles.

Behind him he heard a cry: 'Albeson I'm stuck! Albeson! Help!'

Then there was a metallic banging, as though Nobbler was beating at the hole in his efforts to hit Smithie. There were cries of pain, too, and excited yelps from the dog. Albeson's heart was hammering. He put his head down and went like the wind.

Chapter 13

Albeson ran for a very long time, until his throat was hot and dry and he was gasping painfully. The rain had stopped sometime during his flight, but he was soaked. It was warm wet, maybe rain, maybe sweat he wasn't sure. He stood in the entrance to a back alley for a while to try and get his breath back. In the light from a dim street lamp he could see steam rising from his clothes.

It was after his lungs had got more or less back to normal that Albeson looked carefully about to see where he'd got to. He recognised the dockland streets near the Camber without surprise. They were totally deserted, not a car or a cat stirring. He listened, raising his head to the breeze. Still quite a loud hum of traffic not far off. It couldn't be the middle of the night then. It was cool and very fresh now, all traces of thunder gone. He sucked in great gouts of clean air, cooling rapidly. It was nice.

Albeson cast around in his mind for what to do next. Smithie had been caught, no doubt of that. There was nothing he could have done to have saved him, so he didn't feel bad about it. You couldn't fight an armed man with a fierce dog and that was that. What would they do to Smithie? How long would it be before he told them Albeson was the other culprit? Would he crack under torture? In any case, thought Albeson, they knew already. His mum and dad would have called the police to look for him by now. He felt a cold hand clutch his heart – what if his father got to him first! He felt like running till he found a police-man and giving himself up. But they'd take him home for starters he supposed, before sending him to jail. Whatever happened he was for it. Ah well, he'd just have to stay away. What else could he do? A midget lorry driver's mate? He snorted. He'd no chance without Smithie, no chance. But what else could he do?

Kicking his toes, thinking gloomy, miserable thoughts, Albeson arrived at the Camber. He turned right onto the quays, wandering round by the gaggle of moored yachts and inshore fishing boats. If Jan the Dutchman's boat was there, with its long overhanging foredeck, he could sleep under that if need be. But the old wooden tub was moored off, along-side a half-built torpedo boat opposite the shipyard. He walked slowly along the coal quay, under the high mobile cranes. Drips of dirty rainwater fell into his hair. Albeson shivered. He was getting dead chilly.

As he turned left at the end of the first quay, he saw that the lights were still on in the 'Bridge'. There was the sound of a lot of men, low but loud. Every now and again a laugh split the air. The benches outside were soaked, so there were no seamen taking the night air with their beer. Albeson was a little surprised. He'd thought it was well after pub time. But then perhaps they didn't care much, down here. As he walked slowly past he looked at the lighted windows. They were misty and he could imagine the warmth inside. That man who'd bought him his crisps and liquid lunch. He drooled at the thought. A packet of crisps. He'd give his left arm . . .

Past the pool of light that spilled onto the puddled quayside, a black shape loomed into the air. As his eyes got used to the gloom Albeson thought he recognized the high flare of the bows. He went closer. It was the *Carrie*. The white letters, picked out on that proud glistening bow, were as mysterious as ever. But he'd know her anywhere. The *Carrie* from Newcastle.

For a while he forgot the chill, and the hunger, and all

the other things. He prowled along in the darkness, keeping close into the wall of the fruit warehouses, studying the lovely lines of his favourite ship.

She was quite still in the black waters of the Camber, with hardly any lights on. The barking of her diesel donkey-engine echoed among the dock buildings as the wind pulled the noise this way and that. Every now and again Albeson got a whiff of fresh diesel oil, then a smell of exhaust fumes. He walked slowly along, from the high bow with its winches, down past the low waist, a jumble of derricks and cables, towards the break of the bridge, that rose flush out of the well-deck to form the poop. The cargo hatches were mainly battened down, just one gaping open. *Carrie* was either about to start unloading, or almost ready to sail.

He couldn't guess how long the ship was, but he took quite a time to get past her. He knew she wasn't big, as ships go. Not like some of the big ones you could see if you stood on the beach with the holiday-makers, the ocean liners and that. Or the supertankers. She wasn't even as big as the Navy ships that filled the harbour. About as long as a submarine, perhaps. But a completely different kettle of fish. He scorned submarines. *Carrie* was beautiful, a real sea-going boat. She'd survive anything, whereas a submarine looked like a tube of toothpaste or a cigar. Built for going under. The *Carrie* was built to ride to the waves, to rise over them and crash down, chucking great gouts of white water out from under her shoulders.

Albeson sat on the wheel of a mobile compressor close by the warehouse and studied her rounded stern. There were lights in the afterhouse, shining across the passage-way and out onto the quay through the big square ports cut in her poop side. But he couldn't see anyone, not even a watchman at the head of the rickety old gangplank tied to her rail. The bridge wings were dark too. No one up there having a quiet smoke and keeping an eye out. Odd that. He'd always assumed that there'd be a watchman. Anyone could sneak on board from what he could see.

It didn't enter Albeson's head that *he* could sneak on board until a steel door in the afterhouse opened and the cook came out. You could tell he was the cook because he was dirty, and small, and built rather like a rat with sandy whiskers. Also he had on a white apron, and his grubby tee shirt was stained with sweat. He walked out of the light and disappeared into another door in the forward part of the afterhouse, under the bridge wing.

Out of the door he'd left wide, poured a smell that nearly killed Albeson. It was hot fat. Hot chip fat. He could practically hear them sizzling and bubbling. The idea came into his mind without him being able to stop it. He dribbled so hard and so suddenly that he had to spit. He wanted worse than he'd ever wanted before. Almost without him knowing it he moved quickly and silently towards the gangway. One fearful glance all round the quay. Still deserted. He crept up the swaying planks.

The noise in the alleyway was much louder than he'd bargained for – the donkey-engine must be close by. He felt afraid, exposed. But the smell streaming from the galley was too much for him. He darted to the doorway and jumped over the steel sill.

Inside it was hot and smoky. The first thing he saw was a sort of range, in shining steel, with two vast open pans on it. They had wire baskets, and golden chips writhed in the boiling fat. Beside the pans were three huge kettles, with steam just starting to push out of their spouts. He glanced about, dribbling down his chin now. On the table a real mountain of bread and marge. Beside the mountain another one – of crisp brown chips.

Albeson leapt on the chips as if his life depended on it. He took a great handful and crammed them into his mouth. He almost shrieked. They burnt! He spat them out onto his hand and blew frantically to cool them. He seized a slice of bread and stuffed it in whole. Using both hands he loaded his mouth like a stoker shovelling coal, using the bread to protect it from the hot chips. He glared at the door all the while as though the very strength of his stare could stop the cook from coming back.

It didn't, of course. He'd only swallowed about three mouthfuls – big ones though, that felt like lumps of red-hot barbed wire going down – when he heard the bridge door clang. Ratty was obviously coming back.

When he'd gone up the gangplank into the galley, he'd hardly been thinking. Certainly the idea of how he'd escape if cornered hadn't entered his starving head. But now Albeson stood petrified. He suddenly realized what he'd done. He couldn't believe it. On top of everything else, to be caught stealing food. From his favourite ship too! It was only seconds before the cook appeared, but in that time Albeson had frozen like a frightened rabbit, looked about like a cornered mouse, and shot through the opposite galley door like a shot from a gun. He hadn't even noticed it when he came in, but there it was, wide open and as welcome as it was unexpected. Ships were wonderful things!

Albeson leaned against the cool steel of the afterhouse, just beside the galley door. He heard the cook enter, whistling between his teeth. He didn't appear to have noticed anything, the whistling never faltered. When Albeson's breath was about back to normal he looked for a way to get off the *Carrie*, to escape back to the quayside.

The alleyway was quite light, so he wanted to get out of it as quickly as possible. The other side of the Camber was only a stone's throw away. If anyone came along for a stroll, or if there was a police or security patrol, he'd be spotted in short order. He could either go forward, towards the bow, or aft. If he went forward he'd have to climb down a ladder to the well deck and cross in front of the bridge to reach the gangplank. If he went aft he'd be in an alleyway all the way round, more or less protected from watching eyes. But if the cook hadn't closed the starboard galley door he'd have to pass it and risk being seen. It was only seconds since Ratty had gone back into his den, but Albeson couldn't remember if he'd heard the steel door close or not.

In the end he went aft, picking his way carefully past the bits of metal that stuck out at all angles in the most unlikely places. He'd never have believed there could have been so much gear lying around, ready to trip you. Once he banged his shin against some mooring bitts and nearly cried out. But he didn't; he wasn't that daft!

All the way round the stern he crept, straining his eyes in the gloom to make sure he wasn't seen or he didn't bash into things. He was very nervous, panting a bit. His mouth was burnt too. When he stopped to listen and look he sucked at a piece of skin that hung in a long curtain from the top of his mouth. It was sore. Still, his stomach was better. He could almost feel the hot chips and bread lying in it. He was sure he could feel a burnt patch halfway down his chest, inside, where they'd gone down.

The galley door was closed. He could hear the little ratty man whistling away inside. Such a lot of chips and bread. It must be supper time. Albeson wished he could have suppers like that. Tonight especially a supper like that would have gone down a treat. He bet sailors didn't have to worry how much tomato sauce they were allowed.

Almost as soon as he realized it was supper time, Albeson realized he was in trouble. Getting from the quay up the gangway to the galley had taken no time at all; he hadn't even noticed it. But now he was trying to get away the distance was a pretty fair one. He had to creep, to be invisible, to use the shadows. As he reached the break of the poop, as he reached the ladder that led down to the well-deck and the gangplank, he froze like a rabbit once more.

From out of the 'Bridge Tavern' there was pouring a thick mass of men. They were singing loudly and drunkenly, with shouts and laughs thrown in for good measure. Groups were going off in several directions from the main bunch, some to parked cars, others down the road beside the pub or along both branches of the quay. One of the biggest groups, spreading out like a moving inkblot, was heading for the *Carrie*. Straight as a finger it pointed towards the gangway. Even if he ran Albeson would not reach the bottom before the first seaman did.

He stood there for ages. Time had stopped. The first man, a huge black man in a tartan shirt and baggy blue trousers, stepped onto the planks. They sagged and rattled as he climbed up them. He was puffing like a grampus. Albeson turned and fled.

In the dark, in his fear, he forgot the mooring wires and tripped over them. He flew through the air and smashed into the rise of the stern. He cut his mouth open; a fierce burst of pain shot up from his knee all through his body. He clenched his teeth, crying silently, as he crept round the curve of the afterhouse. Once out of sight of the alleyway he half crawled, half scrambled, without the foggiest idea of where he was going. He could hear a jumbled noise as more and more men climbed the steps into the poop alley and made for the galley to get their supper. He couldn't pick out any words at all because he wasn't really listening. He was in terror. If they found him he would die, something terrible would happen. He whimpered and crawled, scrambled and sobbed.

Out of the darkness rose a brown steel thing that was very like a coal scuttle. There was a door in it held closed by a big clip. Albeson bashed at it frantically with his fist. The clip held, his fist hurt as though he'd broken it. Footsteps. Men were coming aft. They'd hang about in the stern, looking over the black water, to eat their chips. They'd get him. He seized the clip with both hands and wrenched with all his might. It slipped down. The metal door swung open.

Albeson scrambled over the sill and almost fell into the black hole. He was very lucky that his leg slipped between the rungs of a vertical ladder and held him. He turned himself the right way up and started to go down the ladder. It was an amazing distance until his feet touched solid plating.

He lay in a heap in the greasy darkness, his blood hammering. He was so thirsty! He looked up. The door had swung to, but a gleam of light showed round the edges. Where he was, all around him, the blackness was so intense that he could almost feel it. He put his hand in front of his face. But it could not be seen, not even an outline. He had never dreamed that such darkness existed.

Above his head the jumble of noise grew louder. The crew were taking the air as they took their supper. There were clankings and laughter and shouts. Gradually the voices became separate, distinct. Gradually it dawned on Albeson that even when only one voice was going at once he couldn't understand a word that was being said. Gradually it dawned on him that the *Carrie* of Newcastle could not be what she claimed to be. She could not possibly be an English ship. But how? Smithie had read the name dozens of times. Smithie had identified the red black and orange houseflag she wore instead of the Red Ensign.

The thought entered his mind slowly, but he recognized immediately that it was the truth. Smithie could not read either. Nipper, he thought bitterly, you've hit the nail right on the head. Smithie's done you!

A voice above him said something which caused the other men to shout with laughter. Then came a reply. Most of it might have been Greek for all Albeson knew. But the first three words came through as clearly as if they'd been read to him from a page of his comic.

'Donner und Blitzen,' said the man, then jabbered on till there was another loud laugh.

The *Carrie* of Newcastle was a German ship.

Chapter 14

Five minutes later, strangely enough, Albeson was fast asleep. It was probably due to a combination of things – his fear, his exhaustion, the lateness, the few mouthfuls of food he'd managed to cram down to his rumbling stomach. It was also due to the warm refuge he found after he'd discovered *Carrie*'s terrible secret.

Before the German had finished talking Albeson had skidded to his feet at the bottom of the ladder and blundered away into the blackness. He banged his legs and face badly again, but he hardly noticed the pain. Every second he was expecting the Germans to sense his presence, to chase and kill him. As it happened he went in the right direction. He stumbled through an opening in the cool metal and found himself in a sort of room, hardly bigger than a cupboard. It had a small porthole, of thick and filthy glass, which let in a faint trickle of light from the other side of the Camber. In a corner was a pile of canvas and cotton waste. He dropped onto it, his heart hammering, his eyes tight shut.

It was very hot in the cubbyhole. He had been awake for longer than he could guess. It had been quite a day, one way and another. Although his mind was racing, although he was trying to plan his escape, although all sorts of lurid thoughts were crowding each other around and around in his skull, Albeson slept. He jerked awake a couple of times as he slipped off, but it couldn't be helped. His knees came up, his fist balled itself into his mouth, he slept.

When Albeson awoke, there was much more light coming through the port. He stared around him for a while, his eyes glued up with sleep, unable to remember where he was. A square green room with piles of ragged canvas and a coil of steel rope. He came awake with a sickening rush as the deck under him suddenly began to vibrate wildly and a deafening row that he didn't recognize crashed onto his ears. It went on for a long time, really hurting him. They were sinking! They must be sinking!

Gradually the intense noise faded. It was replaced by a steady throbbing, loud but bearable. The deck shivered in a sort of set pattern, you could almost see the regular vibration run across it. They had started up the main engine.

Albeson lay still and listened. Over the beat of the diesel he could hear a confusion of things. Shouts, bangings, a sudden sharper engine roar outside his porthole. He clambered onto the canvas pile, scrabbling for a fingerhold. He rubbed at the dirty glass with his hand and looked out.

The Camber was in full swing. Almost within touching distance one of the small but powerful motor boats that handled the ships in the cramped little commercial harbour seemed to be getting in position to help a ship. A big lad in a blue jersey, not much more than Smithie's age, was standing on the foredeck with a heaving line coiled in his left hand. As Albeson stared he divided the coil and hurled part of it upwards towards the *Carrie.* It dawned on him that the ship to be helped was this one. *Carrie* was about to put to sea. With him on board.

Albeson squeaked with panic and jumped off the canvas to the deck. He reached the doorway before he stopped. He didn't know what to do. He was trapped. But he had to get off, he had to make the quayside before they took him . . . where? To Germany? He went giddy with shock.

The steel door in the coal scuttle thing was wide open, letting in a stream of light. Albeson looked in horror at the greasy ladder he'd so nearly fallen down the night before.

It was a fantastic drop. He'd have broken his neck for sure. Then he saw what lay right aft, a few feet from where he'd wandered in the pitch dark trying to get away from the threat of the Germans. It was a weird thing like an engine, all jagged bits completely unprotected by rails or anything. If he'd walked into it he'd have been carved into little pieces.

As he looked the thing burst into life with a clattering roar that made him leap into the air. Chains led out of it into the blackness right in the stern. They moved, causing a groaning creak from some tortured piece of metal. It must be the steering engine. That contraption was moving the rudder.

Again the deck plates under Albeson's feet leapt wildly. Almost at the same time the note of the engine got louder and deeper. He actually heard the screw start turning deep in the water under him, the splashing crash-crash as it bit into the sea.

He began to run from side to side of the compartment, whimpering in fear. The *Carrie* was going. They'd take him away. The screw was turning. It couldn't be much longer. He had to get off before she left the dock wall.

He darted at the slippery ladder, started to clamber up it towards the brilliant spill of light. He'd only got a yard or so off the deck when the light faded. He looked up in agony. A man's head and shoulders were thrust into the gap. He was holding a great coil of steel rope. With a grunt he let it drop. It missed Albeson by such a little that he felt the small breeze it made before it smashed onto the deck with the sound of a gun going off. Albeson let go of the ladder with a groan and fell onto the coil. He crawled away towards his cubbyhole, his eyes tightly closed in case another coil was about to crush him to death.

On the pile of canvas again he listened as the main engine throbbed, subsided, throbbed again. Every now and again the deck shuddered as the ship went astern, or ahead, or speeded up. He could feel that she was being turned, manoeuvred, pointed out of the Camber to face the main harbour, then the open sea. Almost without realizing it, Albeson found himself staring out of the porthole.

It was amazing in a way. He'd stood on the dockside so many times watching the blue motor boats push and pull at their big charges like so many terriers worrying a bull. He'd listened to the changing engine notes, watched the puffs of black diesel smoke burst out or die as the main engines were used to help the tugs. He'd felt a surge of joy as the ships had at last been heading fair and square out of the Camber and the hollow throbbing beat had deepened and the screw had settled down to a confident pulse of power. He'd watched the blue motor boats cast off and drop astern, back to their little jetty to wait for the next one needing help.

Now he was seeing it from on board.

Albeson had also made a point of walking along with his favourite ships, following them round the left hand corners of the Camber until he'd been stopped by the waters of Dirty Corner, where the outward bound boats went straight ahead. Then he'd run round the end of Dirty Corner, past the car ferry slip, and across to the other side of Point. If he was quick he could be in the boomyard before the freighter had fully cleared the Camber. He'd watch her make the turn hard to port, watch the sudden increase in her smoke, watch her boom majestically down the narrow entrance to the main harbour and out along the coastline towards the open sea.

Now, for the first time in his life, he saw it from the other side.

His nose was glued to the port. It was marvellous, the way the Camber walls looked as they slid past. It was fantastic, how you could see right up High Street. It was terrific, the little Customs hailing station on its legs, standing right out of the sea. He could even see the Customs officers inside, watching without a word as *Carrie* drummed her way out. One by one all the places he knew from the land slid by. The Round Tower, the Square Tower, the funfair on Clarence Pier, the funny silver domes of South Parade Pier, the miles of shingle beaches where the holiday-makers wasted their time.

In the end the shore was new to Albeson, and pretty boring. Just dull-coloured beaches rapidly dropping away into the distance. So boring, in fact, that his eyes drooped. He may have dozed, he wasn't at all sure. But whether he did or not, however long it took, the realization gradually sank in that there was something funny going on with the boat. He hadn't been thinking of her, or anything for that matter, for a long long time. Yes, he must have slept, for ages. Now it all came back to him.

He sat on the canvas and tried to think. But not only was it just too much for him, he was aware of other nasty things. He was desperately thirsty, but not hungry at all. In fact his stomach was starting to feel most peculiar. And there was definitely something funny going on with the boat.

When they'd cleared the harbour Albeson had been absorbed by the view. The boat had been as steady as a rock for all he knew. But now she was behaving in an odd way that was getting odder. She was moving about in a series of rapid judders that did him no good at all. The deck under him kept lifting him up, while leaving his stomach roughly where it was, then falling into thin air till it stopped with a sickening crash. He stood up in a panic, knowing he was going to be sick. The deck bucked like a bronco and chucked him across the cubbyhole. Albeson spewed where he fell, resting on his knees.

He felt better after that, but not much. It would happen again before long. He stood up again, holding on carefully this time. He had to get out. Fast.

The trip to the ladder was a nightmare. The deck was greasy and seemed to be working like a corkscrew. Luckily the door in the coal scuttle effort was still open, but the light, although it helped, also showed up the murderous thrashings of the steering engine. If he slid or was thrown into that he'd be minced. Albeson gripped every handhold so tightly that his hands hurt. He had to steel himself for ages for the last rush to the ladder. Several feet of open plating with nothing to grab at all. One big buck from the ship and he'd take a header straight into the clanking, roaring monster.

He made it at last, wrapping himself round the vertical ladder like a coat of paint. He was panting, ill with a mixture of terror and seasickness. Whatever happened when he reached the top would just have to happen. He couldn't stand it down here a moment longer.

As he climbed, the *Carrie* did her level best to finish him off. Each rung was an individual battle. He used everything except his teeth and eyebrows to get up there. Strange thoughts raced through his head every time he rested. Some madman must have come down in the night and greased the rungs! It was impossible that a ladder should normally be like this! Seamen must all be crazy!

It came as a great shock to Albeson when he stuck his head out of the doorway to find that the sun was shining brightly and there was a fresh warm breeze blowing. The motion of the boat seemed almost to have stopped. He lay over the sill, exhausted and sweating. He was black, covered in grease and muck, and his hands and arms were shaking with effort. Slowly his breath came back to normal. The fresh clean air, unmixed with the stink of diesel, blew the sick feeling out of him.

After a good while he crawled right out onto the deck, where he lay for a few more minutes. Then he stood up, looking out of a square window cut into the stern. There was sea, nothing but sea, stretching away to the horizon. The land was gone. The sea was brilliantly green, not high at all. The storm he'd suffered below didn't exist! He shook his head, baffled. He breathed in great gushes of the clean air. It was damp. He licked his lips. They were salty. He was hungry. He was starving!

Albeson looked around. He was right in the stern, a sort of spade-shaped space behind the afterhouse. To left and right the alleyways led off forward. Just up the alleyways, he knew, were the doors to the galley. His mouth watered. Whatever else he had to do, he had to eat and drink. He started to creep towards the starboard alleyway.

He poked his head round the corner first. Just an eye. Nobody there. He sneaked his whole body round. The galley door was open, pinned back to the afterhouse wall with a clip. One, two, three quick bounds and he was in.

Albeson's eyes shot to the table that had been loaded with chips the night before. He did not even give the rest of the galley a glance. Which was a pity, because when the man spoke to him, he almost died of fright.

The man presumably spoke in German, but Albeson understood all right.

The man just said: 'Hey!'

Albeson's mouth fell open. He stared. Sitting at the other end of the galley, the man stared back. He was black, with a frizz of white hair. He was enormous, with a huge pot belly sticking over the belt of his blue trousers. He was bare from the waist up, with white curly hair on his chest. He was very ugly. He was the man Albeson had seen the night before, the first one up the gangplank.

They both got their wits back at the same instant, but Albeson was out of the galley first. He shot along the alleyway to the break of the poop. He stood at the top of the ladder, the whole length of the ship stretched out before him. There was a man on the deck below about to climb the ladder. He looked very shocked when he saw Albeson above him.

Albeson stood like a statue, holding the rail. The man, another giant but white this time, with huge bushy eyebrows and lots of curly blonde hair, stared upwards.

It was as though a bomb was going off. He could feel the whole of his inside sort of churning, as though *him*, *Albeson*, was going to burst out of his own mouth and escape, leaving his body like an empty sack. He was going to fly away, his soul or something wanted to get out.

He did not recognize his own voice when he spoke. It was a strangled wail.

'Are you a German?' he said.

The black man behind him seemed to speak into his ear.

'Fee, Fie, Fo, Fum!' he said.

The eyes in the face below him rolled right back until only the whites showed under the awful shaggy eyebrows. With a snarl the man threw back his head and bellowed: 'I smell the blood of an ENGLISH man!'

He stepped back from the ladder, yelling with laughter. Albeson closed his eyes and jumped.

He bounced off the rail, off the man, off the hatch-coaming. He landed on his hands and feet together. He didn't know what he was doing, where he was going. He raced forward, a jumble of shouts following.

At the forward end of the hatches another German came at him. Albeson dodged left, running across the green tarpaulin coverings. He crouched behind the winch, then scuttled up the steep ladder to the forecastle. He stood on the foredeck, looking down. Several men were running towards the ladders. The black man was nearest. He looked up at Albeson and shouted 'Hey!' once more. He was grinning from ear to ear. With his white hairy chest he seemed to Albeson to already have a bib on. He could imagine him with a knife and fork poised to start eating him. The man began to climb the ladder.

Straight in front of Albeson, as he faced the stern, the foremast rose like a yellow column. It had steel hoops set into it, like a monkey-ladder. And like a monkey Albeson launched himself onto it and started to climb. As he got higher the shouts from below changed. They sounded worried, afraid. He thought he heard a thick voice say 'Come down, little boy, come down.' He climbed on, his teeth clenched.

When he reached a great metal band around the mast Albeson stopped and looked down. He was dizzy. The deck seemed miles below. Up here the motion of the sea that had made him sick in his cubbyhole had come back in full force. He lurched in great sweeps, jerking at the end of each roll. Around the foot of the mast faces stared up at him, hands waved him to come down. He ignored them. He hung on, panting.

A couple of minutes later one of the men started to climb after him. It was the curly giant who had said the rhyme about the blood of an Englishman. Albeson didn't stop to think. He left the mast and shinned out along the derrick.

The derrick jutted out from the steel column like the jib of a crane. It was thin, and pointed towards the stern, towards England. There were wires along it, used for hauling cargo about with. Albeson moved quickly, his heart thumping, blind to his danger. The derrick swung wildly. Bits of ragged wire cut his hands and legs. He glanced downwards. The blonde German had stopped. The faces below him seemed white. Some mouths were open but he couldn't hear anything. The roaring of the wind filled his ears and his mind.

When he had climbed some way out, Albeson had only enough strength to hang on. The motion was unbearable. He was jerked from one side of the boat to the other, and each time the derrick was brought up short by its wires he was almost flung overboard. Like everything else on board it seemed to have a fine covering of extra-slippy grease. He was as sick as a dog, he wanted to die. But still he held on.

Underneath him there was a never-ending scurry of activity. Every man on board appeared to be there, including some in uniforms and white caps. Things were shouted at him through a megaphone but he heard nothing except the pounding of his blood and the rushing of the wind. By the time his hands gave way there was a curious pile of gear on the hatch-tops and the deck. Blankets, cushions, nests of rope, anything that might break his fall.

He fell a long way and he fell fast. But to Albeson it was like a slow motion film, the deck and the sea spinning and flashing as they climbed towards him. He remembered Smithie, flying through the air to meet the lamp post that ruined his life. He smashed into the deck. Poor old Smithie.

Chapter 15

Poor old Smithie. The strange thought came back to Albeson a lot during the long, hot, boring days as he lay in his hospital bed back in England. For Albeson hadn't been killed, nor did he reckon he'd ruined his life, although he certainly wouldn't be doing much running about or stuff like that for a good time to come. He'd knocked himself around a fair amount and he'd got a lovely scar that ran from the corner of his mouth to his cheekbone. The X-ray girl had also discovered he had a broken foot, although it felt no worse than any of the other battered bits. But the mad feeling of terror and misery he'd been living through seemed to have gone away completely. It was as though something had broken. In the end he decided it was a bit like being on a helter-skelter in a nightmare. He'd been going in a spiral, faster and faster, deeper and deeper into trouble. Then suddenly, just like that, without him knowing how or why – it had stopped. He lay in the white bed, in the stuffy ward, and wondered what had happened.

On the wall beside him there was a picture and a cutting out of the *Evening Echo*, held on the green paint with sellotape. It showed him, Albeson, on a stretcher, surrounded by people. His mum and dad were there, and Derek, with a smarmy grin at getting into the act, and lots of others. Albeson was smiling a rather wobbly smile, all ears and bandages.

The nurses read it out to him so often that he almost

knew it by heart. The headline said: 'Brave stowaway Jimmy comes home – to hospital.' And it gave a brief account of the 'plucky little schoolboy' who'd stowed away by accident, and how glad everyone was to see him back again, safe and sound.

While he was being interviewed at the Camber Albeson had realized very quickly that there were certain things he wasn't supposed to mention. The reporter, a young sallow bloke with spots who blew smoke in his face, had asked how it all started. But when Albeson began to actually say, his father went deep red and shouted at the reporter. Albeson was glad. The very thought of what he'd been doing in the last couple of weeks made him feel hot and frightened. Later in the interview he mentioned Smithie. His father looked at him angrily, but the reporter just cleared his throat and asked a different question, as if Albeson hadn't spoken. It was confusing, but he got the message: you didn't talk about Smithie, and he, Albeson, had somehow become a hero.

So much had happened while he'd been away that he latched on to the idea quite happily at first. It was nice to be a hero, even if he could hardly believe it. He'd been expecting just the opposite, to say the least. So it wasn't till much later, when hospital had become boring and the good things had sort of drifted away into the back of his memory, that he tried to work out what it all meant. He didn't fully understand it, but somehow his feelings about a lot of things had changed. He couldn't put his finger on anything definite, but the changes were there. Strangest of all was the business of the Germans.

The truth of the matter was, that in the few days after the accident, he'd made friends with them. Not just like you sometimes were with grown-ups, but really matey. He liked them. He wanted to talk to them. They had a lot of laughs together.

Even when he woke up for the first time to find the terrifying black man sitting beside him in the sick-bay on the ship, even when he realized he was strapped down in the narrow cot-like bunk, he hadn't expected to be eaten. Somehow or other all that had slipped away into the past.

He looked at the fat, ugly seaman, who hadn't noticed he was awake yet, then said weakly: 'Can I have a drink, Mister?'

The giant jumped like a nervous kitten. Albeson giggled, then gasped aloud. Wow! That hurt! A monster smile spread over the face opposite. Even his nose had hairs growing out, white as snow. Dead funny.

'So. The little boy lives eh?' He spoke English with a daft sort of accent. But he spoke English. Fee, Fie, Fo, Fum!

'Please can I have a drink, sir?' said Albeson.

'Sir! Sir! Ho ho, that is very nice little boy! I thanks you very much. Sir! Ho ho!'

Still laughing he poured Albeson a plastic mug of water, plus two ice-cubes he got from a fat polythene box. He held it to his lips, supporting his head with a big black hand. As Albeson sipped – even the tiny sips hurt like anything – the man said: 'My name is Karl, you get it? Like in English you say Charlie, eh?'

'I didn't know there was any such thing as a black German,' said Albeson.

Karl laughed some more. He laughed practically all the time, it turned out.

'Nah, that's right maybe,' he said. 'Me I'm Portugal mainly. Portuguese yes you call it? My real name you wouldn't understand nor these silly Krauts neither, so they say Karl. You call me Charlie eh?'

He put in the crack about 'silly Krauts', Albeson could see, because the door had opened and the bushy-eyed man had crunched himself into the tiny sick-bay. Two giants in one box, *and* the two who'd nearly scared him daft. He didn't feel a trace of fear. They looked nice. He became aware of the motion of the ship. That felt good too. He was sore all over and it even hurt to breathe too deeply, but Albeson felt good. Very good. Happy as a sandboy.

Helmut was the blonde man's name. He shook hands solemnly (but very gently) with Albeson, and told him in English only slightly crazier than Charlie's that he was sorry if he'd frightened him. Albeson denied it. Briar Boys didn't frighten easy. And no one could say he wasn't a fully-fledged Briar Boy now; just let them try! Both men were pleased with his denial. They smiled all over their faces.

They smiled even more when he told them how he'd first known they were Germans.

'Some man say "Donner und Blitzen" on this ship? I can't believe it true! Usually they say much much worse thing to swear eh? They must have know we have little boy who stow away!'

They chatted on for a while, pausing every now and then when the strain of thinking in English became too much for the men. They sometimes spoke in German to each other, which seemed to relax them. Albeson decided he'd learn German when he got back to England. It sounded good.

Later on Charlie called in the first officer, to show him how Albeson was 'alive and kickering' as he put it. He was called Willi Schmidt, small, blonde, and very young. He didn't look much older than Derek. About twenty or twenty-two perhaps. He spoke almost perfect English.

Willi explained that they had not put back to England when Albeson had fallen because they had not been able to find where he came from. They'd radioed, but no reports of a missing boy had come through. That gave him a funny feeling in his stomach; hadn't anyone even noticed?

'You were very lucky you see, Yimmy,' Willi Schmidt went on. 'You fell onto the mattress from the captain's very own liddle bed. All right, so you also hit the hatchway and the side deck a liddle, but you really ought to be dead.'

The ship had been to four British ports in a very short time. With no idea which one Albeson had stowed away from, and with his injuries obviously not *too* serious, the captain had thought it best to keep him safe and comfortable in their sick-bay. They'd be hitting England again very soon, and the captain, it later turned out, was a great one for letting things sort themselves out in their own time, anyway.

'He thought perhaps a liddle sea voyage would do you good eh?' Schmidt laughed. He whipped down the covers and plunged a hypodermic syringe into Albeson so fast that he could only squeak. The man was a magician! Where had that come from? Schmidt smiled, tucking the covers back firmly. 'You sleep now eh, Yimmy? That fat black man will look after you.' Their smiles became wobbly in front of his eyes. He slept.

All sorts of questions lurked in Albeson's mind, but he was soon great friends with Charlie and Helmut, so could ask them anything. First of all, of course, what was the ship called?

Her name was *Carlotta*. He thought about it when he was on his own. Not as good as *Carrie*? Not at first, but it grew on him. As to the Newcastle bit, well, Albeson never got that. Each time he asked where she came from they told him. But it was a German name that he couldn't make head or tail of. When Helmut wrote it down he studied it carefully and nodded and smiled. But he couldn't read it so it didn't help.

The second thing that Albeson wanted to know, a day or so later, was why all the Germans could speak English. He'd met the captain by now, and the radio operator, and most of the deckhands. Hardly any of them who couldn't get by in a short chat. Alone with Charlie and Helmut he put the question. Charlie laughed.

'Because the German is such a ugly language ja? Like the sound of the pigs who grunting!'

Helmut smiled but was more serious.

'Perhaps it because you English so good people,' he said earnestly. 'You go about in the world many years. You wins the two wars. With Germany. Ja?'

Surprisingly, Albeson blushed. He'd always been convinced that the British were the best. This made him uneasy though. He liked Helmut. He liked all the Germans. He didn't feel better at all. Charlie saw that he was shy. He flicked Albeson's nose with his big square finger.

'Never mind, little boy,' he said. 'There is another reason. I tell you. We are seamen yes? We sails the sea. Now, when you go for be a seaman, when you big little boy, ten years time maybe, you find this: on board of ships, English, Chinese, Dutch, Kraut, Cyprus, there is two language speak. You know what?'

Albeson shook his head.

'Is English, and is Spanish. Them the two language, ja, Helmut? English and Spanish. All seamen, they get enough to take orders in them two, or one of them. Ja?'

Albeson thought about that.

'Maybe you got better schools than us though,' he said. 'Nobody gets taught nothing in England, it seems to me.'

They laughed.

'Good joke,' said Helmut. 'Oh you a very funny little boy, Albeson.'

He hadn't been joking, but never mind. He loved to make them laugh. And now they called him Albeson. They were his special friends. His mates.

Finally Albeson asked about going to sea. He'd made up his mind now. There was no doubt. He would become a seaman. But he wanted to sail with them. He put the question carefully, making sure they understood.

When he was old enough he would go sea, ja? Ja; they nodded. But he wanted to sail with them, Charlie and Helmut, ja? Ja ja! They smiled fit to bust, shipmates mit Albeson, ja! But surely, he said slowly, this ship, *Carlotta*, she is German. I am English. Can I work on the German ship, ja?

Charlie, big ugly Charlie, stood on tiptoes and paraded round the tiny sick-bay like a fashion model, one plate-like paw delicately behind his silver-frizzled black head.

'Am I a German?' he said. 'Not likely I'm not! To be a German is to talk like a pig! Not on your belly I'm not a German! Would I eat cabbage all day? Never!'

Helmut said: 'Seamen are of no country, Albeson. We loves the world. We loves every country ja? And we loves all the person in it, do you understands?'

'Ach so!' yelled Charlie, doubling up over the sick-cot. 'And especially the womens. Ach, Albeson, how we loves the womens!'

They laughed together, happy and rich. They were shipmates.

On the quayside, as he was loaded into the ambulance after the interview, Albeson had cried like a baby. So had Charlie, that was one thing. Helmut kissed both his cheeks and gave him his work-knife in its handmade leather sheath. The captain tucked a rolled-up sea chart in the blankets and told Albeson that when he was better he was to come for a real trip, not to be stuck in the sick-bay like a landlubber. He'd share a cabin with his 'fat friend Karl and zat lazy dumplink Helmut'. As they sped to hospital he felt odd, crying like a stranger as his mum and dad sat on the seat opposite looking strained. At last mum broke down and their tears mingled. She smelt warm and nice and he hugged and hugged her. His father patted his leg and looked embarrassed – but pleased as well.

He wasn't in for all that long. Mainly just observation and the broken bone. Mum came every day and Deena came once but screamed the place down. This was because Albeson, who was meant to keep pretty still, managed to reach out of bed and pull her hair, hard. She'd been telling him what Binnsie and Billy Todd had been putting round the school about what was going to happen when he got back. Mr Johnson had got in a new order of canes, special ones that could cut you to the bone, and he was going to hit him until he begged for mercy. Albeson was gripped with sudden terror, although the bored look on mum's face as she glanced through a magazine didn't change. He'd grabbed Deena's hair, mum had belted him, the chief nurse lady had told her off and Albeson had yelled in agony. Deena didn't come again.

On the whole it was very restful, but he wasn't half bored. The feeling of being a hero wore off surprisingly fast, even with the cutting to remind him.

He learned from Derek, who popped in a couple of times, that Smithie had been sent away, as everyone had always said he should be.

'Sent away?' said Albeson, and the vague, frightened feeling crept back deep in his stomach. 'Sent away where?'

He didn't really want to know, that was the strange thing. Lying in the clean, hard bed, looking at his brother's grinning face, he knew that he didn't want to know. He remembered that night in the rain; the yells, the bangs, the brown and white dog barking fit to bust. He'd run off. And Smithie had been sent away.

But Derek didn't exactly tell him. The grin disappeared and he got quite savage as he ranted on. Smithie was a menace, he said, and ought to be put down. If dad ever got hold of him, that's all! Or Derek, for that matter! When he'd cooled down a bit, Albeson pointed to the cutting on the wall. He wanted to ask why; why he was in the paper and Smithie had been sent away. But he didn't know how.

Derek laughed.

'Yeah, that's good ain't it, Jim,' he said. 'Trust you to come off all right. You know what they say, don't you? Never take no notice of what you reads in the paper! That reporter nearly wet himself when old dad looked like he'd thump him! Best way though eh? Least said soonest mended.'

Albeson didn't argue, but when he thought about it, it seemed unfair, daft. Smithie was all right, he'd been a good mate. Why should he get all the stick and Albeson get nothing? But if you went into that sort of thing too closely, it was a racing cert something like it would happen to you. Better to keep your mouth shut. No point in stirring up trouble.

There was a chance, of course, that they were just waiting till he got better. That Mr Johnson and his new canes, like Deena said; he'd really bash her in when he got out, that was for sure. But he didn't really think so. He looked at the picture on the wall. He was a hero. It said so. So Smithie? Somehow Smithie was a villain . . . He wondered about it quite a lot, for quite a long time, but there was no sense to it at all. One thing was sure though – nothing would keep his mate down for long. If Smithie was in prison, even, he'd bust out. Maybe he'd end up to be a midget lorry driver's mate after all, or they'd go to sea together; yes, that would be fantastic! But after a while he forgot Smithie, he just faded from his mind.

He thought a lot about Pam, too. He reckoned she wasn't *really* a witch, that was just crazy. But her spells were great, no getting away from that. Of course, she'd turned out to be a real rat, in the end, dropping them in it and then leaving them to starve and all. But it made him smile, to think of her all dirty and freckled in those crazy old clothes. Maybe she was a rat, and yellow like Smithie said. Maybe she was. But a thought kept coming back to him, more and more as the days dragged by: he'd see her soon. They'd play, and cast spells, and go to Flathouse and the Camber. Yeah, that would be good. And it was the holidays, too, in a while.

Another daydream that Albeson had quite a lot in the last bit before he went home was about the Germans, about Hans and Erica. He sat in the deck-chair in the hospital garden 'taking the sun' and he dreamed Mrs Armstrong came up behind him. She was nervous, and smiling a funny little smile. The conversation was different every time, of course, but what happened was that she'd brought them to see him. She expected him to be terrified, to jump up and run off screaming or something. But Albeson just smiled. He wanted to meet the Germans now, he wanted to very much. He liked Germans.

And the boy, Hans, who looked somehow like Charlie,

only white and a little boy, said: 'Hello, Yimmy. My name is Hans. How do you do?'

And the girl, Erica, who looked like Pammy, however hard he tried to make her not, said: 'Hello, Yimmy. My name is Erica. How do you do?'

And Albeson said proudly: 'Guten Tag. You can call me Albeson.'

But of course, they never came.